CROWN PRINCE, PREGNANT BRIDE

BY
KATE HARDY

This is a work of fiction. Names, characters, places, locations and
incidents are purely fictional and bear no relationship to any real
life individuals, living or dead, or to any actual places, business
establishments, locations, events or incidents. Any resemblance is
entirely

First p...lished in Great Britain 20...
by Mil... & Boon, an imprint of Ha...lequin (UK) Limited.
Eton H...se, 18-24 ...

ISBN: 978-0-263-24283-6

Harlequin (UK) Limited's policy is to use papers that are natural,
renewable and recyclable products and made from wood grown in
sustainable forests. The logging and manufacturing processes conform
to the legal environmental regulations of the country of origin.

Printed and bound in Great Britain
by CPI Antony Rowe, Chippenham, Wiltshire

Kate Hardy lives in Norwich, in the east of England, with her husband, two young children, one bouncy spaniel, and too many books to count! When she's not busy writing romance or researching local history she helps out at her children's schools. She also loves cooking—spot the recipes sneaked into her books! (They're also on her website, along with extracts and stories behind the books.) Writing for Mills & Boon® has been a dream come true for Kate—something she wanted to do ever since she was twelve. She also writes for Medical Romances™.

Kate's always delighted to hear from readers, so do drop in to her website at www.katehardy.com

Recent books by Kate Hardy:

BEHIND THE FILM STAR'S SMILE
BOUND BY A BABY
A DATE WITH THE ICE PRINCESS*
THE BROODING DOC'S REDEMPTION*
BALLROOM TO BRIDE AND GROOM
ONCE A PLAYBOY*
THE HIDDEN HEART OF RICO ROSSI†
DR CINDERELLA'S MIDNIGHT FLING*
THE EX WHO HIRED HER†

*In Mills & Boon® Medical Romance™
†In Mills & Boon® Modern™ Romance

This and other titles by Kate Hardy are available in eBook format from www.millsandboon.co.uk

With special thanks to Mike Scogings for sharing his expertise on stained glass, and to C.C. Coburn for the lightbulb about the mermaid.

CHAPTER ONE

She wasn't supposed to be there.

OK, Lorenzo knew that tourists were important. Without the income they brought when they visited the house and gardens of Edensfield Hall, his old school friend Gus would never have been able to keep his family's ancient estate going. Even keeping the roof of the house in good repair ate up huge chunks of the annual budget, let alone anything else.

But there were set times when the estate was open to the public. Right now wasn't one of them; the house and gardens were supposed to be completely private. Yet the woman in the shapeless black trousers and tunic top was brazenly walking through the grounds with a camera slung round her neck, stopping every so often to take a picture of something that had caught her eye. At that precise moment she was photographing the lake.

Strictly speaking, this was none of his business and he should just let it go.

But then the woman turned round, saw him staring at her, and snapped his photograph.

Enough was enough. He'd insist that she delete the file— or, if the camera was an old-fashioned one, hand over the film. He was damned if he was going to let a complete stranger make money out of photographing him in the grounds of Edensfield, on what was supposed to be private time. A couple of weeks to get his head together and prepare himself for the coronation.

Lorenzo walked straight over to her. 'Excuse me. You just took my photograph,' he said, not smiling.

'Yes.'

At least she wasn't denying it. That would make things easier. 'Would you mind deleting the file from your camera?'

She looked surprised. 'What's the problem?'

As *if* she didn't know. Lorenzo Torelli—strictly speaking, His Royal Highness Prince Lorenzo Torelli of the principality of Melvante, on the border between Italy and France—was about to inherit the throne and start governing the kingdom next month, when his grandfather planned to abdicate. There had been plenty of stories about it in all the big European papers, all illustrated with his photograph, so no way could she claim she didn't know who he was. 'Your camera, please,' he said, holding his hand out.

'Afraid not,' she said coolly. 'I don't let people touch the tools of my trade.'

That surprised him. 'You're actually admitting you're a paparazzo?'

She scoffed. 'Of course I'm not. Why would the paparazzi want to take pictures of you?'

She had to be kidding. Did she *really* not know who he was? Did she live in some kind of bubble and avoid the news?

'I don't like my photograph being taken,' he said carefully. 'Besides, the estate isn't open to the public until this afternoon. If you'll kindly delete the file—and show me that you've deleted it—then I'll be happy to help you find your way safely out of the grounds until the staff are ready to welcome visitors.'

She looked at him and rolled her eyes. 'I'm not doing any harm.'

Lorenzo was used to people doing what he asked. The fact that she was being so stubborn about this when she was so clearly in the wrong annoyed him, and it was an effort for him to remain polite. Though he let his tone cool by twenty degrees. 'Madam, I'm afraid the house and grounds simply aren't open to visitors until this afternoon. Which means that right now you're trespassing.'

'Am I, now?' Those sharp blue eyes were filled with insolence.

'The file, please?' he prompted.

She rolled her eyes, took the camera strap from round her neck, changed the camera settings and showed the screen to him so that he could first of all see the photograph she'd taken, and then see her press the button to delete the file from her camera's storage card. 'OK. One deleted picture. Happy, now?'

'Yes. Thank you.'

'Right.' She inclined her head. 'Little tip from me: try smiling in future, sweetie. Because you catch an awful lot more flies with honey than you do with vinegar.'

And then she simply walked away.

Leaving Lorenzo feeling as if he was the one in the wrong.

The man was probably one of Gus's friends; he looked as if he was about the same age as Lottie's elder brother. And maybe he'd meant to be helpful; he'd clearly been trying to protect the family's privacy. Indigo knew she should probably have explained to him that she was a family friend who happened to be working on the house's restoration, not a trespassing tourist. Then again, it was none of his business what she was doing there, and his stick-in-the-mud attitude had annoyed her—especially when he'd accused her of being a paparazzo.

She'd only taken his photograph because she'd seen him striding around the grounds, scowling, and he'd looked like a dark angel. Something she could've used for work. It had been a moment's impulse. An expression on his face that had interested her. Attracted her. Made her wonder what he'd look like if he smiled.

But the way he'd reacted to her taking that photograph, snarling about people taking his photo without permission… Anyone would think he was an A-list celeb on vacation instead of some dull City banker.

What an idiot.

Indigo rolled her eyes again and headed for the house. Right now, work was more important. They were taking the window out of the library today and setting it in the workroom Gus had put aside for her in Edensfield Hall. Indigo had already made a short video for the hall's website to explain what was happening with the window, and she'd promised to write a daily blog with shots of the work in progress so the tourists could feel that they were part of the restoration process. And she didn't mind people coming over and asking her questions while she was working. She loved sharing her passion for stained glass.

And the stranger with the face of a fallen angel—well, he could do whatever he liked.

Lorenzo was still slightly out of sorts from his encounter with the paparazzo-who-claimed-she-wasn't by the time he went downstairs for dinner. When he walked into the drawing room, he was shocked to see her there among the guests. Except this time she wasn't wearing a shapeless black top and trousers: she was wearing a bright scarlet shift dress, shorter than anyone else's in the room. And they were teamed with red shoes that were glossier, strappier and had a higher heel than anyone else's in the room.

Look at me, her outfit screamed.

As if anyone would be able to draw their eyes away from her.

Especially as her hair was no longer pulled back in the severe hairdo of this afternoon; now, it was loose and cascaded over her shoulders in a mass of ebony ringlets. All she needed was a floor-length green velvet and silk dress, and she would've been the perfect model for a Rossetti painting.

Lorenzo was cross with himself for being so shallow; but at the same time the photographer was also one of the most beautiful women he'd ever met. He couldn't help acting on the need to know who she was and what she was doing here.

He just about managed a few polite words with Gus before drawling, 'So who's the girl in the red dress?' and inclining his head over towards the trespasser, as if he wasn't really that interested in the answer.

'Who?' Gus followed his glance and smiled. 'Oh, that's Indigo.'

How could Gus be so cool and calm around her? Lorenzo wondered. The woman made him feel hot under the collar, and he hadn't even spoken to her yet this evening.

'A friend of the family?' Lorenzo guessed.

'She's one of Lottie's best friends from school.'

Which was surprising; Indigo didn't look as if she came from the same kind of titled background that Gus and his sister did.

'Actually, she's here on business, too; she's restoring the stained glass in the library for us,' Gus explained. 'My mother's asked her to work up some ideas for a new stained-glass window, so she's been taking photographs of bits of the estate.'

Which explained why she saw her camera as one of the tools of her trade. Lorenzo felt the colour wash into his face. 'I see.'

'What did you do, Lorenzo?' Gus asked, looking amused.

'I saw her taking photos this afternoon and I thought she was a trespasser. I, um, offered to help her find her way out of the grounds,' Lorenzo admitted.

Gus laughed. 'I bet she gave you a flea in your ear. Our Indi's pretty much a free spirit. And she really doesn't like being ordered about.'

He grimaced. 'I think I'd better go and apologise.'

'Good idea. Otherwise you might be in danger of getting an Indi Special.'

'An Indi Special?' Lorenzo asked, mystified.

'Indi. Short for Indigo, not for independent. Though she's that, too.' Gus raised an eyebrow. 'Let's just say she's an original. I'll let Lottie introduce you.' He caught his sister's eye and beckoned her over. 'Lottie, be a darling and introduce Lorenzo to Indi, will you?'

'Sure. Have you two not met, yet?' Lottie tucked her arm into Lorenzo's and led him over to Indigo to introduce them. 'Indi, this is Lorenzo Torelli, a very old friend of the family.' She smiled. 'Lorenzo, this is Indigo Moran, who's just about the coolest person I know.'

Indigo laughed. 'That's only because you live in a world full of stuffed shirts, Lottie. I'm perfectly normal.'

Lorenzo looked at her and thought, no, you're not in the slightest bit normal—there's something different about you. Something *special.* 'Gus said you were at school with Lottie,' he said.

'Until she escaped at fourteen, lucky thing.' Lottie patted Indigo's arm. 'Indi was brilliant. She drew caricatures of the girls who bullied me and plastered them over the school. It's a bit hard to be mean when everyone's pointing at you and laughing at your picture.'

Indigo shrugged. 'Well, they say the pen is mightier than the sword.'

'Your pen was sharper as well as mightier,' Lottie said feelingly.

Now Lorenzo understood what an 'Indi Special' was. A personal, public and very pointed cartoon. And he had a nasty feeling what she'd make of him, given what she'd said to Lottie about coming from a world full of stuffed shirts.

'Can I be terribly rude and leave you two to introduce yourselves to each other properly?' Lottie asked.

'Of course,' Indigo said.

Her smile took his breath away. And Lorenzo was surprised to find himself feeling like a nervous schoolboy. 'I, um, need to apologise,' he said.

She raised an eyebrow. 'For what?'

'The way I behaved towards you earlier today.'

She shrugged. 'Don't worry about it.'

But he did worry about it. Good manners had been instilled into him virtually from when he was in the pram. He was always polite. And he'd been rude to her. 'I didn't realise you were a friend of the family, too.' He looked at her. 'Though you could have explained.'

'Why? For all I knew, you could've been a trespasser, too.'

'Touché.' He enjoyed the fact that she was back-chatting him. After all the people who agreed with everything he said and metaphorically tugged their forelocks at him, he found her free-spirited attitude refreshing. 'Gus says you're restoring the glass in the library.'

'Yes.'

'Forgive me for saying so, but you don't look like...' He

stopped. 'Actually, no. Just ignore me. I'm digging myself a huge hole here.'

She grinned, and the sparkle in her eyes made his pulse speed up a notch. 'I don't look like a glass restorer, you mean? Or I don't look the type to have been at school with Lottie?'

Both. Ouch. He grimaced. 'Um. Do I have to answer that?'

She looked delighted. 'So, let me see. Which shall we do first? School, I think.' Her voice dropped into the same kind of posh drawl as Lottie's. 'I met her when we were eleven. We were in the same dorm. And unfortunately we shared it with Lolly and Livvy. I suppose we could've been the four musketeers—except obviously I don't have an L in my name.'

'And it sounds as if you wouldn't have wanted to fight on the same side as Lolly and Livvy.'

'Absolutely not.' Her eyes glittered and her accent reverted back to what he guessed was normal for her. 'I don't have any time for spitefulness and bullying.'

'Good.' He paused. 'And I hope you didn't think I was bullying you, this morning.'

'If you'll kindly delete the file,' she mimicked.

He grimaced. How prissy she'd made him sound. 'I did apologise for that.'

'So are you a film star, or something?'

'No.'

'Well, you were acting pretty much like a D-list celeb, trying to be important,' she pointed out.

Should he tell her?

No. Because he didn't want her to lose that irreverence when she talked to him. He didn't think that Indigo Moran would bow and scrape to him; but he didn't want to take that risk. 'Guilty, m'lady,' he said lightly. 'Are you quite sure you're a glass restorer and not a barrister?'

She laughed. And, oh, her mouth was beautiful. He had the maddest urge to pull her into his arms and find out for himself whether her mouth tasted as good as it looked. Which was so not how he usually reacted to women. Lorenzo Torelli was always cool, calm and measured. He acted with his head rather than his heart, as he'd always been brought up to do. If you stuck to rigid formality, you always knew exactly where you were.

What was it about Indigo Moran that made him itch to break all his rules? And it was even crazier, because now absolutely wasn't the time to rebel against his upbringing. Not when he was about to become King of Melvante.

'I'm quite sure I'm a glass restorer. So were you expecting me to be about forty years older than I am, with a beard, John Lennon glasses, a bad haircut and sandals?'

Lorenzo couldn't help laughing. And then he realised that everyone in the room was staring at them.

'Sorry. I'm in the middle of making a fool of myself,' he said. 'Not to mention insulting Ms Moran here at least twice.'

'Call me Indigo,' she corrected quietly, and patted his shoulder. 'And he's making a great job of it,' she cooed.

'I, for one,' Gus's mother said with a chuckle, 'will look forward to seeing the drawing pinned up in the breakfast room.'

Indigo grinned. 'He hasn't earned one. Yet.'

'I'm working on it,' he said, enjoying the banter. How long had it been since he'd been treated with such irreverence?

Though a nasty thought whispered in his head: once he'd been crowned, would anyone ever treat him like this again, as if he was just an ordinary man? Would this be the last time?

'Indigo, may I sit with you at dinner?' he asked.

She spread her hands. 'Do what you like.'

Ironic. That was precisely what he couldn't do, from next month. He had expectations to fulfil. Schedules to meet. A country to run. Doing what he liked simply wasn't on the agenda. He would do what was expected of him. His duty.

CHAPTER TWO

WHEN THEY WERE called to dinner, Lorenzo switched the place settings so he was seated next to Indigo.

'Nicely finessed, Mr Torelli,' she said as he held her chair out for her.

Actually, he wasn't a Mr, but he had no intention of correcting her. 'Thank you,' he said. 'Your name's very appropriate for a stained-glass restorer.' Not to mention pretty. And memorable.

'Thank you.' She accepted the compliment gracefully.

'So how long have you been working with glass?'

'Since I was sixteen. I took some evening classes along with my A levels, and then I went to art college,' she explained.

Very focused for someone in her mid-teens. And hadn't Lottie said something about Indigo leaving their school at the age of fourteen? 'So you always knew what you wanted to do?'

She wrinkled her nose. 'It's a dreadfully pathetic story.'

'Tell me anyway,' he invited. 'It'll make me feel better when you savage me in one of your cartoons.'

'I was sent away to boarding school at the age of six.'

Lorenzo had been five years older than that when he'd been sent away, but he remembered the feeling. Leaving home, the place where you'd grown up and every centimetre was familiar, to live among strangers. In his case, it had been in a different country, too. With a child's perception, at the time he'd thought maybe he was being sent away as a punishment—that somehow he'd been to blame for his parents' fatal accident. Now he knew the whole truth, and realised it had been his grandparents' way of giving him some stability and protecting him from the potential fallout if the press had found out what had really happened. But it had still hurt back then to be torn away from his home.

'I hated it,' she said softly.

So had he.

'I cried myself to sleep every night.'

He would've done that, except boys weren't allowed to cry. They were supposed to keep a stiff upper lip. Even if they weren't English.

'The only thing that made school bearable was the chapel,' she said. 'It had these amazing stained-glass windows, and I loved the patterns that the light made on the floor when it shone through. I could just lose myself in that.'

For him, it had been music. The piano in one of the practice rooms in the music department. Where he could close his eyes and pretend he was playing Bach at home in the library. 'It helps if you can find something to get you through the hard times,' he said softly.

'I, um, tended to disappear a bit. One of my teachers found me in the chapel—they'd been looking for me for almost an hour. I thought she'd be angry with me, but she seemed to understand. She bought me some colouring pencils and a pad, and I found that I liked drawing. It made things better.'

He found himself wanting to give Indigo a hug. Not out of pity, but out of empathy. He'd been there, too. 'Why did you decide to work with glass instead of being a satirical cartoonist?' he asked.

'Drawings are *flat*.' She wrinkled her nose. 'But glass… It's the way the colour works with the light. The way it can make you feel.'

Passion sparkled in her dark blue eyes; and Lorenzo suddenly wanted to see her eyes sparkle with passion for something else.

Which was crazy.

He wasn't in the market for a relationship. He had more than enough going on in his life, right now. And, even if he had been thinking about starting a relationship, a glass artist with a penchant for skewering people in satirical cartoons would be very far from the most sensible person he could choose to date.

Besides, for all he knew, she could already be involved with someone. A woman as beautiful as Indigo Moran would have men queuing up to date her.

'You really love your job, don't you?' he asked.

'Of course. Don't you?'

'I guess so,' he prevaricated. He'd never known anything else. He'd always grown up knowing that one day he'd become king. There wasn't an option not to love it. It was his duty. His destiny. No arguments.

'So what do you do?' she asked.

She really wasn't teasing him, then; she actually didn't know who he was. And he wasn't going to make things awkward or embarrass her by telling her. 'Family business,' he said. 'My grandfather's retiring, next month, so I'm taking over running things.' It was true. Just not the whole truth.

'Workaholic, hmm?'

He would be. But that was fine. He'd accepted that a long time ago. 'Yes.' Not wanting her to get too close to the subject, he switched the topic back to her work with glass.

* * *

When he smiled, Lorenzo Torelli was completely different. He wasn't the pompous idiot he'd been in the garden; he was beautiful, Indigo thought.

And she was seriously tempted to ask him to sit for her. He would be the perfect model for the window she was planning.

'If you're really interested in the glass,' she said, 'come and have a look at my temporary workshop after dinner.'

'I'd like that,' he said.

They continued chatting over dinner, and Indigo found her awareness of Lorenzo growing by the second. It wasn't just that she wanted to sketch him and paint him into glass; she also wanted to touch him.

Which was crazy.

Lorenzo Torelli was a total stranger. Although he seemed to be here on his own, for all she knew he could be married. And her radar to warn her that a man was married or totally wrong for her hadn't exactly worked in the past, had it? She'd made the biggest mistake of her life where Nigel was concerned.

Though at the same time she knew it wasn't fair to think that all men were liars and cheats who just abandoned people, like her ex and her father. Her grandfather hadn't been. Gus wasn't. And, from what Lottie had told her, their father had been a total sweetheart and had never even as much as looked at another woman. Though Indigo still found it hard to trust. Which was why she hadn't even flirted since Nigel, much less dated.

'Penny for them?' Lorenzo asked.

No way. She fell back on an old standby. 'When I'm about to start work on a new piece, I tend to be pretty much in another world.'

'There's nothing wrong with being focused on your work.'

Good. She was glad he understood that.

After coffee, he asked, 'Did you mean it about showing me your work?'

'Sure.' She took him through to the library. 'I guess it starts here. We took the window out this afternoon.'

'There's a facsimile of the window on the boards,' he said, sounding surprised.

'People come especially to Edensfield to see the mermaid window. I don't want to disappoint them by hiding everything behind scaffolding,' she explained. 'I went to Venice when they were doing some work on the Bridge of Sighs, and they'd put a facsimile of the bridge on the advertising hoardings. I thought that was a brilliant idea and I've tried to do something like that with my own work, ever since.'

'Good idea,' he said.

'Come and see the mermaid up close. She's gorgeous. Victorian—very much in the style of Burne-Jones, though she isn't actually one of his.'

He smiled. 'I was thinking earlier, if you'd been wearing a green velvet dress, you would look like a PRB model.'

'Thank you for the compliment.' She blushed, looking pleased. 'That's my favourite art movement.'

'Mine, too.' He almost told her that his family had a collection and that Burne-Jones had sketched his great-great-grandmother. But then he'd have to explain who he was, and he wasn't ready to do that yet.

'I'd love the chance to work on some PRB glass.' She gave a wistful smile. 'Maybe one day.' She led him into a room further down the corridor. 'Gus set up this room as my workshop. Obviously we've had to rope off my table for health and safety purposes—I work with dangerous substances—but people can still talk to me and see what I'm doing. I have a camera on my desk and the picture feeds through to that screen over there, so they can see the close-up work in total safety.'

She was so matter-of-fact about it. 'Don't you mind working with an audience?' he asked. 'Doesn't it get in your way?'

'The house is only open for a few hours, four days a week,' she said with a shrug. 'The visitors won't be that much of a distraction.'

The window from the library had already been dismantled into frames; the one containing the mermaid was in the centre of her table.

'I took close-ups of the panel this afternoon so I have a complete photographic record,' she said. 'Next I'm going to take it apart, clean it all and start the repairs.'

'Which is why the camera's one of the tools of your trade.' He understood that now. 'I'm sorry I accused you of being a pap.'

'You've apologised—and nicely—so consider it forgotten.' She looked at him. 'Though if you really want to make it up to me, there is something you could do.'

Quid pro quo. It was a standard part of diplomacy. Though part of Lorenzo was disappointed that she'd asked. He'd thought that Indigo might be different. But maybe everyone had their price, after all. 'Which is?'

'Would you sit for me?'

He blinked. 'Sit for you?'

'So I can draw you.'

He'd already worked that out. 'Why?'

She spread her hands. 'Because you look like an angel.'

Heat spread through him. Was this her way of telling him that she was attracted to him? Did she feel the same

weird pull that he did? 'An angel?' He knew he was par-
roting what she said, but he didn't care if he sounded dim.
He needed to find out where this was going.

'Or a medieval prince.'

That was rather closer to home. Though he thought her
ignorance about his identity was totally genuine. 'And what
would sitting for you involve?' he asked.

'Literally just sitting still while I sketch you. Though
modelling is a bit hard on the muscles—having to sit perfectly still and keep the same expression for a minimum of
ten minutes is a lot more difficult than most people think.
So I'd be happy to compromise with taking photographs
and working from them, if that makes it easier for you.'

Which was where this had all started. 'Is that why you
took my photograph?'

She nodded. 'You were scowling like a dark angel. You
were going to be perfect for Lucifer.'

'Why, thank you, Ms Moran,' he said dryly.

She grinned. 'It's meant as a compliment. Or you could
be Gabriel, if you'd rather.'

'Didn't Gabriel have blond hair?'

'In the carol,' she said thoughtfully, 'his wings were
drifts of snow, his eyes of flame.'

On impulse, he sang a snatch of the carol.

Her eyes widened. 'I wasn't expecting that. You have a
lovely voice, Mr Torelli.'

'Thank you.' He bowed slightly in acknowledgement
of the compliment.

'So will you sit for me?'

He was tempted. Seriously tempted. But it was all too
complicated. 'Ask me another time,' he said softly. When
he'd worked out how to say no while letting her down gently. 'Tell me about your work here. The mermaid's face is

damaged, so are you going to replace that bit of the glass with a copy?'

'I could do, but that would be a last resort. I want to keep as much of the original glass as possible.' She grimaced. 'I'd better shut up. I can bore for England on this subject.'

'No, I'm interested. Really.'

'Trust me, you don't want to hear me drone on about the merits of epoxy, silicon and copper foil,' she said dryly.

He smiled. 'OK. Tell me something else. What's the story behind the mermaid?'

She raised an eyebrow. 'Gus hasn't told you?'

'It's not exactly the kind of thing that comes up when you're a schoolboy,' he said, 'and since we left school I guess we've had other things to talk about.'

'Rebuke acknowledged,' she said.

He wrinkled his nose. 'That wasn't a rebuke.'

Maybe not. It hadn't been quite like the way he'd spoken to her in the garden, when he'd been all stuffy and pompous.

'Tell me about the mermaid,' he invited.

He really meant it, she realised in wonder. He actually wanted to hear what she had to say. 'So the story goes, many years ago the Earl was a keen card-player. He won against almost everyone—except one night, when he played against a tall, dark stranger. It turned out that the stranger was the devil, and his price for letting the earl keep the house and the money he'd wagered and lost was marriage to the earl's daughter. The earl agreed, but his daughter wasn't too happy about it and threw herself into the lake. She was transformed into a mermaid and lived happily ever after.'

'I thought mermaids were supposed to live in the sea,' Lorenzo said.

She grinned. 'Tut, Mr Torelli. Hasn't anyone told you that mermaids don't actually exist? Lottie says there's a version of the story that has the mermaid rescued by a handsome prince, but that might be a bit of a mix-up with the Hans Christian Andersen story.'

'I hope not, because if I remember rightly that doesn't have a very happy ending.'

Lorenzo's eyes were very dark. Beautiful. She itched to paint him, to capture that expression. If only he hadn't said no. Or maybe she could paint him from memory.

He reached over and wound one of her curls round the end of his finger. 'I can see you as a mermaid, with this amazing hair floating out behind you,' he said softly.

Oh, help. That sensual awareness of him over dinner had just gone up several notches. It would be so easy to tip her head back and invite him to kiss her…but that would be such a stupid thing to do.

Indigo was about to take a step backwards. Just to be safe. But then Lorenzo leaned closer and brushed his mouth against hers.

His kiss was sweet and almost shy at first, a gentle brush of his mouth against hers that made every single one of her nerve-ends tingle. And then he did it again. And again, teasing her and coaxing her into sliding her hands into his hair and letting him deepen the kiss.

Indigo had had her fair share of kisses in the past, but nothing like this. Even Nigel, the man she'd once believed was the love of her life, hadn't been able to make her feel like this—drowsy and sensual, and as if her knees were going to give way at any second.

When Lorenzo stopped kissing her, she held on to him, not trusting her knees to hold her up. The last thing she wanted to do was fall at his feet and make an idiot of herself.

Though she had a nasty feeling that she'd already done that.

'We really ought to get back to the others,' she said.

'Are you worried that they'll think you lured me here for other reasons than to talk about glass?'

'No.' She could feel the colour seeping into her face. 'Don't be ridiculous. They all know how I am about my work. They probably think I'm boring the pants off you right now.'

He gave her a slow and very insolent smile. 'Interesting choice of phrase, Ms Moran.'

Her face heated even more. Because now she could see herself taking his clothes off. Very, very slowly. And not because she wanted to paint him naked: because she wanted to touch him. Skin to skin. Very, very slowly. Until he was begging her for more.

Oh, for pity's sake. She'd only just been introduced to him. Insta-lust wasn't the way she did things. Why was she reacting to him like this? 'Let's go back,' she said, hoping she didn't sound as flustered as she felt.

'Has Indi been showing you what she's doing with the mermaid?' Gus asked Lorenzo when they rejoined the others in the drawing room.

'Yes.'

'She's brilliant. Maybe you ought to commission her to do you a portrait for the coronation. Glass instead of oils,' Gus suggested.

Indigo frowned. 'Coronation? Whose coronation?'

Gus looked embarrassed. 'Whoops. I think I might have just put my foot in it.'

'It's fine,' Lorenzo said.

Oh, no, it wasn't, Indigo thought. There was a lot more to this than met the eye. Especially as Lorenzo looked shifty, all of a sudden.

They chatted for a few moments more; when they were alone again, Indigo narrowed her eyes at him. 'What's this about a coronation?'

'The King of Melvante is abdicating next month and handing over to his grandson,' Lorenzo said.

She still didn't get it. Why had Gus suggested that Indigo should do Lorenzo's portrait in glass? 'And?' she prompted.

He wrinkled his nose. 'That would be, um, me.'

'You're going to be the King of Melvante?'

He nodded. 'Nonno's already passed on a lot of his duties to me. And he's going to be eighty, next month. I want him to enjoy his old age, not have the burden of the crown.'

'So that's what you meant about the family business. Being king.'

He shrugged. 'Running a country isn't so different from running a business.'

Even so, she was hurt that nobody had told her. Lottie was her closest friend, and she'd known the family for years. Lorenzo obviously thought that she'd tell tales to the media, but surely Lottie's family knew otherwise?

A king-to-be.

No wonder he'd been sensitive about having his photo taken, and no wonder he hadn't wanted to sit for her.

This changed everything.

When he'd kissed her, only minutes before, she'd thought this just might be the start of something. How stupid of her. No way could a king-to-be have a fling with someone like her. OK, so strictly speaking Indigo's father was an earl, so it wasn't so much the noble and commoner thing; but he'd been married to his countess when Indigo was born and not to Indigo's mother. The press would drag that up if they found out she was even vaguely involved with Lorenzo. Plus there was the whole mess of her relationship with Nigel and the way he'd let her down. That would look bad, too. A king couldn't afford to be touched by scandal.

So her common sense needed to kick back in, and fast. Absolutely nothing was going to happen between them now.

It *couldn't*.

'I'll make sure I address you properly in future, Your Highness,' she said coolly. 'It's a pity you didn't bother to tell me before.'

'It wasn't relevant. You're a friend of the family and so am I. Who we are outside Edensfield isn't important.'

'You still could've told me.'

'How? Was I supposed to correct you and tell you that, actually, no I'm not *Mr* Torelli, and it should be "Your Royal Highness Prince Lorenzo" to you?' He grimaced. 'Talk about an arrogant show-off.'

She blew out a breath. 'I guess you have a point. I understand now why you were annoyed with me for taking your photograph.'

'Because I try to protect my privacy—not because I think I'm a celeb or a special snowflake who deserves red carpet treatment,' he said.

Her frown deepened. 'What about your bodyguards? I assume you have them, and they're so discreet that I haven't noticed them yet.'

'I get a little bit more liberty than usual from my security team because I'm staying in the house of a family friend,' he said.

'But you still can't do anything spontaneous or even go for a walk without telling half a dozen people where you're going. Your life must be scheduled out down to the millisecond.'

'Most of the time, yes,' he admitted. 'But I'm officially

on leave at the moment. Taking a bit of time to get my head in the right place, so to speak.'

'Before you're crowned king.'

'Yes. Obviously I'm not entirely neglecting my duties while I'm here—I can do a lot of things through the internet and the phone—but Nonno thought I needed a bit of time out to prepare myself.'

'Your grandfather,' she said, 'sounds very sensible.' Like hers had been. 'But forgive me for being dim. I don't tend to read the society pages, so I really had absolutely no idea who you were.'

'You,' he said, 'are the last person I'd accuse of being dim.'

'You only met me today. I could be an airhead.'

He raised an eyebrow. 'Give me some credit for being able to judge someone's character quickly and accurately.'

'I guess in your position you have to do that all the time.' She paused. 'So how come you're taking over, and not your father?'

'He died in a car crash when I was ten,' Lorenzo said. 'Along with my mother.'

She could see the pain in his eyes, and then he was all urbane and charming again. Behind a mask. Clearly it hurt too much to talk about. She could understand that; there were certain bits of her own past that she didn't talk about.

'I'm sorry,' she said softly. 'That must've been hard for you. And for your grandparents.'

'It was a long time ago, now,' he said. 'You get used to it.'

'Yes, you do.'

'That sounds like experience talking,' he said.

She nodded. 'My grandparents brought me up.' She couldn't quite bring herself to tell him of the circumstances, not wanting him to pity her.

'Something we have in common,' he said.

Not quite. She didn't think that Lorenzo's parents were

like hers, choosing to abandon their child. In his case, his parents had been taken from him in an accident. In hers, her father had chosen to distance himself before she was born—his only contribution to her life had been to pay for part of her education—and her mother had been more focused on her own love-life than family life. 'Just about the only thing.'

He smiled. 'Sometimes that makes life more interesting.'

And more complicated, she thought. Lorenzo Torelli was gorgeous. The way he'd kissed her earlier had made her bones melt. Which meant she needed to keep a safe distance between them until he left Edensfield for his kingdom. 'I guess I ought to stop monopolising you and let you chat to everyone else. And I have a few things I need to do for work, so I'd better get a move on. Nice to have met you. Good evening,' she said.

He gave her a tiny little smile that very clearly called her a chicken. Guilty as charged, she thought—because he scared her as much as he drew her. She couldn't afford to let him matter to her.

Besides, a man destined to be king would've been taught how to be charming from when he was in the cradle. The attention he'd paid her had been flattery. And she already knew the dark side of flattery—the last time she'd let herself fall for a spiel, it had ended in tears. She'd learned the hard way that relationships let her down, but her work never did.

'Good evening, Indigo,' he said softly, and she fled.

CHAPTER THREE

INDIGO WASN'T IN the breakfast room when Lorenzo came downstairs, the next morning. And when he casually mentioned her name, Gus just smiled. 'She's even more of a workaholic than you are. She'll have been in her workroom since the crack of dawn.'

Lorenzo knew that he ought to be sensible and avoid Indigo. But the attraction from last night hadn't gone away. So he couldn't resist taking a detour to the kitchen, making her a mug of coffee and wandering casually into her workroom. Just to say hello, he told himself. There couldn't be any harm in that. Could there?

Today Indigo was back to wearing shapeless clothes and having her hair pinned back, and she was also wearing a pair of safety goggles. This had to be the most unsexy outfit in the world. And yet Lorenzo was aware of every drop of blood thrumming through his veins when she glanced up from her work and saw him.

'I thought you might like this,' he said, and handed her the mug. 'Milk, no sugar.'

'Thank you.' She pushed the goggles up on top of her head. 'How do you know how I like my coffee?'

'I noticed yesterday at dinner,' he said. He'd been taught from an early age to notice the details. 'Do you need a hand with anything?' It was a stupid question, and he knew it even as the words came out.

'Thank you,' she said, 'but, apart from the fact that my work needs specialist training, I work with acids, flux, a hot soldering iron, sharp blades and glass—all things that could do serious damage to you.'

'I guess so.'

'Even if I didn't have bad intentions towards you—and, just for the record if you happen to be wired and your security team's listening, I don't—there's still the risk of an accident. My insurance company would have a hissy fit at the idea.'

He liked the fact that she'd clearly thought this through. Though it also surprised him that Indigo Moran had such a deeply conventional side, given the dress she'd worn last night. 'And that bothers you? I thought you had a reputation for being a free spirit.'

'Which isn't the same as being reckless and stupid,' she said. 'What do you expect me to do—jump into a lake and pull you in with me?'

He laughed. 'Point taken. No, I don't think you're stupid.' He paused. 'So can I watch you work, today?' he asked.

She looked surprised. 'Are you really interested in glass, are you being polite, or are you just bored and at a bit of a loose end?'

He liked her plain speaking. But either they could spend all day fencing, or he could come clean. Given how little time he had left here, he chose the latter option. 'It's an excuse to spend time with you. And I have a feeling it might be the same for you, too.'

She looked wary. 'I'm not so sure that it's a good idea.'

At least she hadn't denied that she wanted to spend time with him. So he could be just as honest with her. 'I *know* it isn't a good idea,' he said softly.

She said nothing, just looked even warier.

'If I wasn't who I am, would your answer be different?'

'Probably,' she admitted.

'Do you have any idea how refreshing it was yesterday,' he said, 'to have someone backchat me and treat me like a normal person, for once?'

'Poor little rich boy,' she said, folding her arms and giving him a pointed look.

He grinned. 'And you're still doing it. I like you, Indigo. I think you like me. What's the harm in two people getting to know each other?'

'As you pointed out yesterday, you're used to the paparazzi following you. You have a security team looking after you. You're not just a normal person. If anyone wants to get to know you, or you want to get to know someone, then the whole world will know about it.'

'This is a private house,' he said.

'Which is open to the public,' she reminded him.

'Who won't be expecting to see me—they might think, oh, that man sitting by the table over there looks a bit like that Prince Lorenzo guy, but they'll think no more than that.'

'What if they do recognise you?'

'They won't,' he said confidently. 'It's like when that famous violin player busked on the metro in Washington DC a few years ago, playing a Stradivarius. People weren't expecting a famous musician to be busking on the metro with one of the most expensive instruments in the world, so they didn't recognise him and hardly anyone stopped to listen to what he was playing. It's all about context.'

'You,' she said, 'are just used to getting your own way all the time.'

'Not *all* the time.'

'Did you get an A star in persistence lessons at prince school?' she asked.

He laughed. 'There isn't such a thing as prince school. Besides, you know very well I went to the same school as Gus.'

'In a different country, and when you were still very young,' she said thoughtfully.

'Not as young as you were when you went to boarding school—I was eleven.' And how he'd missed his family. Thought it had been good practice for his stiff upper lip. 'I know this is crazy,' he said. 'I just want to spend a bit of time with you. I have a free day, but I know you're working, so maybe I could make myself useful. Kind of multi-tasking.'

She scoffed. 'You're telling me that a man can multi-task?'

'Don't be sexist.' He grinned at her. 'I learned how to multi-task at prince school.'

She laughed, then. 'Says the man who claims that prince school doesn't exist.'

'They're not formal lessons, exactly, but over the years I've been taught about the importance of diplomacy and how to...' He wrinkled his nose. 'I was going to say, how to handle people, but I think you might take that the wrong way.'

Her blush was gratifying. 'Yes. I would.'

'I don't mean manhandle,' he said softly. 'That's not who I am. I'm not expecting you to fall into my arms because I'm about to become the King of Melvante. But I can't stop thinking about you. And I think it's the same for you, too. That kiss, last night...' He paused. 'I don't behave like that. I don't usually act on impulse and I definitely don't do insta-lust. I'm pretty sure you don't, either.'

'No.' Again, she blushed. Telling him that maybe, just maybe, it was different with him.

'It would be sensible if we just stayed out of each other's way. But I can't do that. Something about you…' He blew out a breath. 'OK. I'll shut up and stop distracting you now.'

'Maybe,' she said quietly, 'if you wear goggles, that'll be enough to disguise you. And you need to wear goggles anyway if you're going to be on this side of the rope. I don't want you to get a glass splinter or dust in your eye. And you need gloves, too, if you're going to work with me.' She reached under her table and rummaged around in a box. 'Try these.'

They fitted perfectly. Which was a sign, of sorts, he thought. 'They're fine.'

'OK.' She handed him a pair of protective glasses, and he put them on.

'What do you need me to do?' he asked.

'Help me clean the lead cames. That'd be easy to teach you.'

'I'd like that,' he said. It was so far away from his normal life that it really was like having a rest.

He watched her work, fascinated by how neatly and quickly she worked to remove the stained glass from the leads without damaging the fragile glass or the soft metal. And he noticed how she labelled everything before putting it in a specific place and then photographing it.

'I assume that's to be sure everything goes back in the right place?' he asked.

She nodded. 'Plus I'm documenting everything that I do, so the next time the glass needs work the restorer will know exactly what I've done and how.'

Her work was methodical, neat and efficient. She was good at giving instructions, too; when she showed him how to clean the leads, she gave him an old piece of lead from her box of tricks under her desk so he could practise first, and corrected his technique without making him feel stupid. Lorenzo liked the fact that she was so direct and clear.

And when the house opened to the public, he discovered that Indigo was far from being the socially inept nerd she'd claimed to be. She was seriously good with people; she was patient, charming, and he noticed that she assessed them swiftly so she could work out whether they wanted a quick and simple answer, or if they'd prefer a longer and more detailed explanation.

Lorenzo noticed how patient Indigo was, never once making her questioners feel stupid or a nuisance. If anything, she went out of her way to make them feel appreciated.

Funny, all the formal training he'd had in diplomacy didn't even begin to approach this. Indigo was a natural with people, warm and open, and the rigidity of boarding school clearly hadn't left its mark on her. Lorenzo knew that she could teach him a lot, just by letting him shadow her. And maybe if he could focus on that, on the way that Indigo could help him prepare for his new role, it would stop him thinking of her in a different context. One that would cause too many problems for both of them.

Once the crowds had left, Lorenzo fetched them both some more coffee.

She looked up at him and smiled. 'Thank you—that's really kind of you. Sorry, I'm afraid I've rather ignored you this afternoon.'

'You were busy working and talking to visitors,' he said. 'And I have to say, I'm impressed by how at ease you are with people.'

She looked surprised. 'But you're a prince. You have to talk to people all the time. Aren't you at ease with them?'

'Not in the same way that you are,' he admitted. 'You

have this natural empathy.' And, because he was so used to formality, he had to work at being at ease with people. Which pretty much negated the point.

'I'm surprised they didn't teach you that sort of thing at prince school.'

He rolled his eyes. 'Very funny.'

'I still think you'd make an awesome model for a stained-glass angel,' she said. 'Though I can understand why you don't want to sit for me.'

'It's not that I don't want to. I *can't*. In another life,' he said softly, 'I'd sit for you with pleasure.' And he'd enjoy watching her sketch him, seeing the way she caught the tip of her tongue between her teeth when she was concentrating. And then maybe afterwards…

'But in this life it'd be a PR nightmare,' she said, going straight to the root of the matter. 'The new King of Melvante has to be squeaky clean.'

'Yes.' Until he'd met Indigo, that hadn't been a problem. But Indigo Moran made him want to break every single one of his rules and then some. To stop himself thinking about it, and to distract her from probing his thoughts too deeply, he made an exaggerated squeaking noise. 'Like this.'

She laughed. And, to his relief, everything felt smooth and light and sparkly again.

'I'd better let you get on. You've had enough distractions for today.'

She smiled at him again. 'You can stay if you want to.'

Tempting. So very, very tempting. And he wanted to spend more time with Indigo. He liked this side of her, the fun and the carefree feeling he didn't normally have time for.

But he really needed to let his common sense get back in charge. Preferably right now. He was supposed to be preparing for his new role, not acting on impulse and indulging himself. 'Thanks, but I'll see you later, OK?' And then, hopefully, the next time he saw her he'd be back in sensible mode and he'd be able to treat her as just another acquaintance. He could be charming and witty, but he could keep his emotions totally in check.

And what he needed more than anything else, right now, was a little time at the ancient grand piano in the library.

Now the visitors had gone and the house was back to being fully private, the family dogs had the free run of the place again, so a couple of minutes after Lorenzo had settled at the piano he discovered that Toto, an elderly golden Labrador he'd known since puppyhood, was leaning against his leg. Just like home, except with a bigger dog, he thought with a smile, and reached down to ruffle the dog's fur. And then he lost himself in the music.

Indigo could hear piano music. Which was odd, because she had a very quiet cello concerto playing on her iPod. She reached over and paused the track, and listened again. Definitely a piano, but not something she recognised.

The piece stopped, and there was silence for a moment, before a snatch of something, and then a pause and a few bars of something else, as if someone was trying to decide what to play next.

Curious, Indigo made sure that all her electrical equipment was turned off and her pots of acid all had lids on, and went in search of the music. As she neared the library, the music got louder. She paused in the doorway of the library. Lorenzo was sitting at the piano; from her vantage point, she could see that his eyes were closed as he was playing.

In another life, she thought, this could've been his career. Though he didn't have the luxury of choice.

When he'd finished, she clapped softly, and Lorenzo opened his eyes and stared at her in surprise.

'What are you doing here?' he asked.

'I heard the music,' she said simply.

He grimaced. 'Sorry. I didn't mean to disturb you.'

'I was going to have a break anyway.' She paused. 'You're very good.'

'Thank you.'

Lorenzo accepted the compliment gracefully, even a little bit shyly. Indigo had the strongest feeling that this was a part of himself that he normally kept hidden. She couldn't resist asking, 'Would you play some more for me?'

'I...' He gave her another of those shy smiles that made her heart contract. 'Sure, if you want. Take a seat.'

She heeled off her shoes and curled up on a corner of the battered leather chesterfield sofa. The Labrador came over and put a paw on one of the cushions, clearly intending to lever himself up next to her.

'Toto, you bad hound, you know you're not allowed on the furniture,' she scolded him.

The dog gave her a mournful look and she sighed and slid off the chesterfield onto the floor. 'All right, then, I'll come down and sit with you.'

He wagged his tail, licked her face and then sprawled over her.

'And you're much too big to be a lapdog,' she said, but she rubbed the dog's tummy anyway and he gave her a look of absolute bliss.

'You like dogs?' Lorenzo asked. Then he rolled his eyes. 'That was a stupid question, because the answer's obvious.'

'I love them. But my work takes me all over the place and not everyone's comfortable with dogs, so I can't have one of my own. I come and borrow Lottie and Gus's every so often.' She paused. 'I see you didn't mind Toto leaning against your leg while you were playing. I take it you like dogs, too?'

He nodded. 'I have dogs at home, but mine are a little smaller than Toto.'

She grinned. 'Prince Lorenzo, please don't tell me you have a Chihuahua.'

'And carry it around with me in a basket?' He laughed. 'No. We have various spaniels. And although they're nearly as old as Toto, they're not quite as well behaved. They sneak up onto the furniture as soon as you've looked away. Especially Caesar. He's my shadow when I'm at home.'

And she could tell that he didn't really mind. Which made him seem so much more human. A king who didn't necessarily expect all his subjects to obey him and would indulge an elderly and much-loved dog.

'What do you want me to play?' he asked.

'Anything you like,' she said, and listened intently as he ran through several pieces.

'That was fabulous,' she said when he'd finished. 'When you said last night that it helped to get through tough times if you had something... It was music for you, wasn't it?'

He nodded, and she had to stop herself from walking over to the piano and hugging him. She didn't want him to think she was pitying him; but she could understand how a lonely little boy, far from his home and his family, needed to take refuge in something. She'd been there herself. 'Did you ever think about being a musician?'

He shrugged. 'It wasn't exactly an option. My job's been mapped out for me pretty much since I was born.'

She frowned. 'Doesn't that make you feel trapped?'

'It's my duty and I'm not going to let anyone down.'

She noticed that he hadn't actually answered the question. Which told her far more than if he'd tried to bluff his way out of it. She knew she'd feel trapped, in his shoes.

Stuck in a formal, rigid culture where you were expected to know every single rule off by heart and abide by them all. Stifling. She'd hate it even more than she'd hated the rigidity of boarding school.

'If you could do whatever you wanted, what would you do?' she asked softly.

'Anything I wanted?' His eyes were very, very dark.

'Uh-huh.'

'Right here and right now?'

She nodded.

'I'd do this.' He got up from the piano stool, walked over to her, drew her to her feet, wrapped her in his arms and kissed her.

Just like last night. Except it was more intense because, this time, she knew how perfectly his mouth fitted against hers. How his touch made her pulse beat faster. How *right* it felt.

Oh, help.

She really didn't want Lorenzo to know how much he affected her. After the way Nigel had betrayed her trust and abandoned her, she didn't want to be that vulnerable ever again. Hopefully being a little sarcastic with him would defuse the situation and make her feel more in control again.

She fanned herself with one hand. 'You're not too shabby at this, Your Royal Highness,' she drawled. 'Did they teach you this at prince school, too?'

He narrowed his eyes at her. 'Indigo, will you please shut up about prince school?'

But her idea of a defence mechanism turned out to be a total failure, because then he kissed her again, tiny nibbling kisses that inflamed her senses and left her breathless. And she ended up kissing him right back.

This had to stop. Now. 'Had a lot of practice, have we?'

It didn't seem to faze him in the slightest. 'That'd be

telling, and a prince should never kiss and tell,' he shot back. 'You talk way too much, Indigo Moran.' He caught her lower lip between his, sending her pulse skyrocketing again. 'But, since you clearly want to talk—let's talk about last night,' he said. 'At dinner. That dress.'

She frowned. 'What was wrong with my dress?'

'Nothing.' He sighed. 'Apart from the fact that it made me want to pick you up, haul you over my shoulder in a fireman's lift, and carry you to my bed.'

Which put another set of pictures in her head.

If he carried on like this, she was going to do something seriously stupid.

'Droit de seigneur?' she asked.

'No.' He kissed her again. 'For the record, I don't believe in forcing anyone to do anything they don't want to do. Being a troglodyte and carrying you off to my bed is—' he licked his lower lip '—well, a fantasy. Which I would only do if you liked the idea, too.'

Now he'd said it like that, she could really picture it. And what would come after, too...

She shivered.

'What's the matter, Indigo?' he asked softly.

'You've just made it hard for me to breathe,' she admitted.

'Good. Now you know how that dress made me feel last night. And your shoes. I noticed just how long your legs are. And if you'd had any idea how much I wanted to touch you...' He traced the outline of her mouth with the tip of his forefinger. It made her tingle all over and she couldn't help parting her lips in response.

And then he actually grinned.

Oh, *really*? she thought. He honestly believed he had more self-control than she did? Well, two could play at that. She held his gaze, then sucked the tip of his finger into her mouth.

Instantly his pupils dilated and there was a slash of colour in his cheeks.

'Touché,' he whispered. 'Indigo, we need to stop this. Now.' He dragged in a breath. 'It wouldn't be fair or honourable of me to lead you on. I'm going back to Melvante soon. My life's going to change out of all recognition.'

Of course it was.

He looked tortured. 'I can't offer you a future.'

'I know. And even if you could, I'd be the worst person you could ask,' she said. What with the scandal surrounding her birth, and the fact that she'd been naive enough to trust Nigel and not work out for herself that he was already married, she was totally unsuitable even to be a king's mistress. 'I take it you need to find yourself a princess.' Which would put her totally out of the running. Not that she wanted the formal, rigid life of a royal family.

He rolled his eyes. 'I probably do have to choose a bride within the next six months, yes. And she probably has to be from a noble family. Though, just for the record, I don't care if your parents aren't aristocrats. It's how you treat other people that matters to me, not how many coronets are in your family tree.'

'Actually, my father's an earl.' He looked surprised, and honesty made Indigo add, 'The problem is, though, he was still married to his countess when he had a fling with my mother and she fell pregnant with me.'

'So that's why you ended up at the same school as Lottie?' he asked.

'It was my father's idea of providing for me,' she said dryly.

'Money instead of attention?'

He'd hit the nail right on the head. 'My father and I are never quite sure if we ought to acknowledge each other or not,' she said. 'I don't want to hurt his family by claiming him as kin—I mean, I'm the child of an affair, and it'd be horrible to rub their noses in that. It wasn't their fault that he behaved badly. So it's easier...' She sighed. 'Well, for me not to acknowledge him and for him to pretend that I don't really exist.'

'But that hurts you.'

Did it still show? Or was Lorenzo just particularly perceptive? She shrugged. 'I'm lucky: my grandparents loved me. I was never deprived of love, if that's what you're thinking.'

'But your grandparents let you go to boarding school at such a young age?'

'They didn't exactly have a lot of choice. My grandmother wasn't very well at the time—they had enough on their plates without having to look after a small child.'

He frowned. 'What about your mother? Why didn't she look after you?'

She blew out a breath. 'You might as well know the worst. When it was obvious that the earl wasn't going to leave his wife for my mother, she left me with her parents and bolted.' She looked away. 'With someone else's husband.'

Lorenzo knew first-hand what kind of damage affairs could cause. Collateral damage, too. His own mother's affair had blown his whole world apart. If she'd been able to cope with life in the royal family, then she wouldn't have had the affair—and his father wouldn't have reacted by driving their car into a wall. And just maybe he would've grown up with both his parents, in a happy family, and it would've been another thirty years before he'd had to think about becoming king.

Or maybe it would've been a different kind of unhappy childhood, with his parents always arguing in private and pretending everything was just fine and dandy where the public was concerned.

Not that he was going to tell Indigo about that. He didn't talk about the scars on his heart to anyone. Ever. 'That's tough on you.'

She shrugged. 'As I said, my grandparents loved me.'

The implication was clear: her mother hadn't. 'Do you see your mother now?'

Indigo shook her head. 'She ended up in a yachting accident with Married Man Number Four. She drowned. All I have of my mother are photographs and some very fleeting memories.'

It was the same for Lorenzo. Photographs and fleeting memories. Except nobody knew the true circumstances of his parents' accident. Nobody except his grandfather and their legal adviser. They wouldn't have told him the truth, except some papers had been misfiled and he'd come across them when he was eighteen and discovered the truth for himself. He'd gone off the rails for a week, shocked to the core that his father could've done something so terrible. The paparazzi had taken a picture of him looking haggard and with the worst hangover in the history of the universe; and then his grandfather had hauled him back to the palace, had a very honest and frank discussion with him, and Lorenzo had reassumed his stiff upper lip.

'That's tough on you,' he said again.

'It was tougher,' she said, 'proving to everyone that I wasn't like my mother.'

Yeah. He knew all about that, too—having to convince his grandfather that he wasn't like his father.

'Especially when I wanted to leave boarding school. But I hated the rigidity of the place, and the sense of entitlement that so many of the girls had.'

'What did you do?' he asked.

'Gave my father a business plan,' she said. 'If I went to a normal state school at the age of fourteen, he'd save four years of fees—which would be enough to buy my grandparents' cottage. If he let them live there rent-free for the rest of their lives, then he'd get his investment back when he sold the cottage. Win-win. He got money, and I got freedom.'

Lorenzo's heart bled for her. How could her father have been so cold-blooded that she had to offer him a business plan as a way out of a school that she hated? 'And he agreed to it?'

'Yes.'

For a second, he saw pain in her eyes.

And then she grinned. 'I told him the alternative was that I'd behave so badly, I'd get thrown out of every boarding school in England. But he knew I was right. And I proved to my grandparents that I wasn't like my mother. I wasn't running away, I was making the right choice. I got a weekend job in the local supermarket as soon as I was old enough, and a bar job to keep me going through art college until I graduated.'

'And you got a First?' he asked.

She inclined her head. 'I made my grandparents proud of me before they died.'

Though her father had obviously not acknowledged her achievements. 'Indi. I'm not pitying you, but right now I want to hug you,' he said.

'It's OK. I'm a big girl. I learned to deal with it years ago.' She shrugged. 'It's the earl's loss, not mine.'

And what an idiot the man was, not realising what a treasure he had in Indigo.

Lorenzo stole another kiss. 'Indigo. Will you please tell me to stop this?'

She kissed him back. 'Colour me bad, Your Royal Highness, but what's the alternative to stopping?'

His breath hitched. 'I think you've just spiked my blood pressure. Are you suggesting…?'

'We both know where we stand. You're about to take over from your grandfather and become king. You don't have time for a relationship. I have an empire to build with my business—I don't have time for a relationship, either.' She paused. This was crazy. But, at the same time, it was safe, because what she was proposing involved a time limit. Which meant she wouldn't get involved with him. 'I'm here until the end of the month. You said you don't have to go back to Melvante for a little while. Are you staying here until you go back?'

'Yes.'

'So we're in a private house. Among friends who would never rat us out to the press. Lottie's my oldest friend, and I'm guessing that Gus is one of your oldest friends, too.'

'He is. And I trust him totally.' He lifted her hand to his face and pressed his lips against her wrist, feeling the way her pulse beat hard against his mouth. Indigo Moran was everything he couldn't have. A breath of fresh air. Vibrant and lively. Totally unsuitable. And he knew without having to ask that she'd hate his world just as much as his mother had. This was never going to work.

Yet, at the same time, neither of them could deny the attraction between them.

'So you're suggesting we have a fling,' he said slowly.

'A *mad* fling,' she corrected. 'Because we both know that, although we're attracted to each other, in the real world we're not remotely suitable for each other. So we go into this with our eyes open. And we both walk away at the end of it. Intact.'

Which told him someone had walked away from her before, and left her very far from intact. 'It feels a bit—well, dishonourable. To offer you just a fling.' Especially now he knew about her background. She was the child of a fling, and she'd paid the price by losing a whole generation of her family.

'Lorenzo, I'm not suitable marriage material for you, so you're not in a position to offer me anything else,' she pointed out. 'Which means either we have to spend the next couple of weeks having a lot of cold showers and trying to avoid each other, or...' Her breath caught. 'Just for the record, I don't normally proposition men.'

He stole another kiss. 'I already know that. Despite that dress you were wearing last night, you're not the type. And I'm very flattered that you should proposition me.'

Her eyes narrowed. 'But you're going to say no.'

'My head's telling me that this is a bad idea,' he said. 'But...' He blew out a breath. 'I don't do this sort of thing, either. I'm just a boring businessman.'

'You're a king in waiting,' she corrected.

'Same difference. Running a country's the same as running a business. It's just a slightly different scale.' He shrugged. 'Indigo, I always act with my head. I think things through and I look at all the options. I never do anything on impulse.' Not since that week of getting seriously drunk—and he hadn't touched brandy ever again after that. 'Yet I can't stop thinking about you. And kissing you just now was more impulsive than I've been in years.' He leaned his forehead against hers. 'Have you ever wanted something so much, you feel as if you're going to implode?'

She didn't answer; and he was pretty sure it had something to do with the man who'd walked away from her.

Which was precisely what he was going to have to do.

And he didn't want to hurt her. Though he had a feeling that it might already be too late for that. She'd been rejected by her father, dumped at boarding school, and left in pieces when someone she loved had walked away from her. The fact that she'd been brave enough to suggest a fling also meant she'd made herself vulnerable.

He pulled back just enough to drop a kiss on her forehead. 'Cold showers and avoidance it is.'

'I'm not so sure that's going to work. I have pictures in my head. And I think you do, too.' She moistened her lower lip with the tip of her tongue, and he was near to hyperventilating. He really wanted to kiss her again.

'Indigo, I'm trying really hard to maintain control, here.'

'What if you didn't have to?' She stroked his face, and he turned his head to press a kiss into her palm. 'What if you could be whoever you wanted to be, just for, say, one night?'

'What scares me,' he admitted, 'is that I don't think one night with you would be enough.'

'A week, then. A fortnight. Maybe until you go back to Melvante. Look, you can still do whatever it is you planned to do here—spending time with Gus, thinking things through, sorting out kingly strategies. And I have work to do on the window. I'm not going to back out of my business commitments.' She paused. 'But, in between the business stuff, there are spaces.'

He could see what she meant. 'Spaces where we can just be.'

'Together,' she confirmed softly.

He sat down on the chesterfield and pulled her onto his lap. 'Your arguments are very persuasive, Ms Moran.'

She inclined her head. 'Why, thank you, Your Royal Highness.'

'Though I still feel dishonourable, offering you nothing but a fling.'

'They're the only kind of terms that either of us is in a position to offer,' she pointed out. 'So it's your choice,

Lorenzo. Cold showers—or this.' She cupped his face in her hands and skimmed her mouth against his.

His lips tingled where her skin touched his, and he couldn't help tightening his arms round her and responding to her kiss in kind.

'This,' he said when he could finally drag his mouth away from hers. *'This.'*

CHAPTER FOUR

ALTHOUGH INDIGO WENT back to her work when she left the library, she found herself stopping often to think about Lorenzo. She still couldn't quite believe what they'd agreed to. Since when did she do anything crazy like this? After Nigel's betrayal and the way her life had collapsed, two years ago, she'd kept all her relationships strictly platonic.

And now she was about to have a mad fling with a man who was about to become king.

Mad being the operative word, she thought wryly.

It took her ages to choose what to wear for dinner. At home, Indigo didn't bother changing for dinner—there wasn't much point when her meal was a hastily grabbed snack and she was going straight back to work for the rest of the evening. But she knew that Lottie's family always dressed for dinner, and when she stayed at Edensfield she always tried to fit in, so as not to embarrass her friend.

Last night's dress had made Lorenzo want to be a troglodyte and carry her off to his room.

Tonight, then, she'd wear something more demure. Something that would give him the chance to change his mind, maybe. Because she was pretty sure that one of them needed a dose of common sense, and right at that moment she didn't think she was the one who'd get it. So she picked a dress that one of her friends from art college had made as a prototype Edwardian costume and then presented to her because it practically had her name written over it: a midnight-blue velvet creation with a high scooped neck and cap sleeves, which came down to her ankles and was teamed with a silk sash in the same colour, a chunky faux-pearl necklace and a matching bracelet.

And hopefully seeing Lorenzo in a dinner jacket—looking a bit too much like the actor who played James Bond for her comfort—wouldn't make her do anything rash…

Lorenzo knew the second that Indigo walked into the room, but he forced himself not to turn round and stare at her.

They hadn't yet discussed whether they were keeping their mad fling just between themselves, so for now he was going to err on the side of caution. Besides, what if she'd come to her senses during the afternoon and had changed her mind?

He played it as cool as he could when Gus beckoned her over to join them. He couldn't read her expression at all. But then, just for a second, she dropped the guard on her gaze and he could see the heat in her eyes. He returned the glance, hoping that she could read exactly the same thing in his eyes, and then they went back to polite, neutral conversation.

Except inside he was far from feeling polite and neutral.

Last night's dress had been the equivalent of a cheeky come-hither whistle.

Tonight's was clearly meant to be demure. Except it wasn't. The velvet dress skimmed her curves and just made him want to see more. And he wanted to undo every single one of the tiny buttons on the back of her dress and kiss each millimetre of skin as he bared it.

Not to mention seeing that glorious hair spread all over his skin.

Right now, he could really do with a cold shower to shock some common sense back into him.

For all he knew, he was speaking utter gibberish and he could barely concentrate on the people he was speaking to. This was insane. He never lost it like this. What was it about Indigo Moran that made him react like this?

It made it worse that he was seated opposite her at the dining table. So near, and so out of reach. He knew it was appallingly rude of him, but he just wanted dinner and all the social chit-chat to be over, so he could be on his own with Indigo and kiss her until they were both dizzy.

'And she drags me off to the most obscure little churches,' Lottie was saying, but her tone was so indulgent that Lorenzo could tell she wasn't really complaining.

'And you love it, because it always means finding a nice little tea-shop nearby afterwards,' Indigo teased back.

'Exactly. It's so civilised. Where would we be without afternoon tea?' Lottie asked. She ruffled Indigo's hair. 'Actually, it's lovely to know someone who can find beauty so easily and help others see it. I'm so going to get you that "vitrearum inconcinna" T-shirt we saw at the stained glass museum that time.'

'Glass geek,' Lorenzo translated with a smile. That would be just about perfect for Indigo.

Indigo gave him a sassy look. 'I'm glad to see that prince school didn't skimp on your education in Latin, Your Royal Highness.'

He coughed. 'Given my native language, it'd be pretty embarrassing if I didn't know any Latin.'

'Though I guess you'd call it *il vetro antico*.'

He inclined his head. 'Or maybe *il vetro artistico*, depending on how old it was.'

Gus topped up their glasses. 'We really should've introduced you two *years* ago. You could've had so much fun out-geeking each other.'

Indigo laughed. 'I'm not that competitive.'

'Yeah, right,' Lorenzo drawled, and she just laughed again.

From the chatter over the dinner table, Lorenzo could see how well Indigo fitted in at Edensfield; she was clearly loved by all the family, not just Lottie, and it sounded as if she was a regular visitor to the estate. He wondered why they'd never met before, given how long they'd both been friends with the family. Maybe they'd just visited the house at different times. But surely she'd been invited to Gus's wedding to Maisie two years ago, when he'd been Gus's best man? Though he didn't remember meeting her then, and he was pretty sure that he would've remembered.

And then he looked up to discover that she was watching him. He raised his glass casually, as if to take a sip of wine, then held her gaze and gave her the tiniest, most discreet toast.

She smiled, and copied his actions.

So she hadn't had second thoughts about their mad fling, then. Good. And funny how it made him feel so warm inside. To the point that, after dinner, Lorenzo let Gus coax him into playing the piano for them. They all crowded into the library round the baby grand, and Lorenzo played the slow bit of Beethoven he'd played for Indigo that afternoon. He hoped she'd work out that he was playing it for her. Would it make her think of the way he'd kissed her afterwards in this very same room? He sneaked a discreet glance in her direction, and the slight wash of colour in her face was gratifying in the extreme. Yup. She was thinking about that kiss, too.

And then he switched to pop, choosing songs that he

knew would get everyone singing. Then he discovered something else about Indigo. Her singing was *terrible*.

But he liked the fact that nobody called her on it. She was just—well, part of the family and accepted as one of them. Something he had a feeling she hadn't experienced that much.

He saw her expression change from pleasure to utter horror, the moment she realised that she was singing aloud, and he had to fight back a smile. Did she really have no idea how cute she was?

'I'm afraid I'm going to be a bit of a party pooper,' she said, when he stopped playing. 'I need to load the photographs I took this afternoon and finish off the restoration blog post for tomorrow morning.'

In other words, she was embarrassed about her singing and was desperate to escape, he thought. How could he tell her that it didn't matter, without bringing up the very subject she wanted to avoid? And if he asked her to stay, he might as well be wearing a T-shirt emblazoned with 'Hey, everyone, I'm interested in Indigo'. Or worse.

Lottie gave her a hug. 'Don't work too hard, Indi. You're not here as our slave, you know. You're here as our friend.'

'I know,' Indigo said. 'But I'm also here to do a job.'

'And you love your job more than anything else.' Lottie ruffled her hair. 'Go be a glass geek, then. See you later.'

According to Lottie, Indigo loved her job more than anything else. Which made Lorenzo wonder again about the man who'd clearly hurt her in the past. Was she using work to block it out? Then again, he didn't have much room to talk. He'd always had workaholic tendencies, too, trying to make up for the way his father had disappointed his grandfather. Which was stupid, because you couldn't make up for someone else. He knew that. But he still couldn't seem to stop himself trying. And Indi had already admitted that she did the same. She was the first person he'd met who really understood what made him tick. Was it the same for her, too?

He stayed at the piano for just long enough to be polite and make it seem that he wasn't following Indigo, and then he headed over to her workroom and leaned against the doorway. To his surprise, she really was typing away on her laptop; so maybe her swift exit hadn't just been an excuse because she'd been embarrassed by her voice.

She looked up and saw him, then gave him a sheepish smile. 'Sorry. I'm an awful singer.'

'Don't apologise,' he said. 'Actually, it was nice that the music carried you away. And you don't have to be perfect at everything, every second of the day.'

'Uh-huh.' But she didn't sound convinced.

Why was she so hard on herself? Was it something to do with the strained relationship with her father? But he had a feeling that Indigo's flaw was the same as his own: she tried to be perfect. When she wasn't, she covered it up by being boho and arty. When he wasn't...well, that didn't happen. He always did the right thing.

Except for this mad fling with her. Which he wasn't going to let himself think about.

'You're busy,' he said. 'I'll leave you be.' He paused. 'Unless you want some coffee.'

'Coffee would be very nice,' she said softly. Then she looked him straight in the eye. 'But you would be better.'

His common sense vanished entirely. 'I'm giving you fair warning that I'm about to switch to troglodyte mode,' he said.

She blushed, just a tiny bit. 'Good. Though you should have noticed that I dressed demurely tonight.'

'I beg to differ.'

'High neckline, low hem.' She gestured to her dress.

'An indigo dress for Indigo.'

'That's what Sally said when she gave it to me. My friend from art school—she was studying textiles. We shared a flat and I sometimes used to model for her.' She smiled. 'It's a copy of an Edwardian design. What's not demure about it?'

'The buttons,' he said succinctly.

'The buttons?'

'The ones down the back of your dress. They make me want to undo them.'

'Oh, really?' She gave him a slow, insolent smile. 'Give me ten minutes to check this and upload it. My room?' Then she paused and looked awkward. 'Wait. Your security team.' She bit her lip.

'Bruno and Sergio? They're discreet. Totally and utterly.'

'It still feels a bit...' She grimaced. 'Well. As if we have an audience.'

'We don't,' he reassured her. 'This afternoon, when I was playing the piano, they knew I was in the library and they left me to it because they knew I needed some space. They didn't see me kiss you then, or the evening before.' He paused. 'I take it you want to keep this just between us?'

She nodded. 'It's a temporary thing,' she said softly, 'and we both know nothing can ever come of it, plus we're both staying at a friend's home. We're not in our own space.'

'If you're worrying about what people might think of you,' he said equally softly, 'I'd say the corridors of this house have seen plenty of people quietly slipping through them in the dead of night to a different bedroom, over the years.'

'I know.' She sighed. 'Sorry, I'm being silly. Not to mention very unsophisticated.'

'No, I know what you mean.' He smiled at her. 'I did wonder if you'd changed your mind.'

'I thought you might've changed yours.'

He shook his head. 'Every time I remember that I'm this sober, sensible and ever so slightly *boring* man, I look at you. And then all I can think is how much I want to kiss you.'

'In that case, it would be terribly rude of me not to let you,' she said.

'I'll see you in ten minutes,' he said. He checked which room was hers and was pleased to find that they were at least on the same corridor. There would be nothing more embarrassing for both of them than for him to be found wandering around on the wrong side of the house—because then Gus and his family would guess exactly what was going on.

Ten minutes later, Indigo was in her room. Adrenalin was fizzing through her veins, and she couldn't sit still; she couldn't even concentrate on browsing through the latest textbook on glass she'd bought before coming to Edensfield, planning to study it in her free time. Instead, she found herself pacing the room and looking at her watch every two seconds.

All she could think about was Lorenzo. The fact that he'd be coming to her room. The fact that they'd be starting their mad fling. And it made her feel like a teenager after her first kiss, light-headed and giddy with desire.

Well, the giddiness had to stop. She was going to enjoy every second of this, but she was also going to keep remembering that this was temporary. No promises on either side. And then they'd both be able to walk away with their hearts intact. She wouldn't be broken and helpless and hurting, the way she'd been after Nigel. She'd be strong and happy and absolutely fine.

There was a soft rap on the door.

Lorenzo.

She could barely get the words out. 'Come in.'

He walked in looking even more like James Bond, still wearing his dinner jacket but with his shirt collar open and his bow tie untied. And he had both hands behind his back, just as you always saw royal men walking. It brought it home to her that she was having a mad fling *with a king-to-be*. How crazy was that?

But then he lifted her up and swung her round before setting her back on her feet. 'Indigo Moran, I've wanted to kiss you all evening.'

'I've wanted that, too,' she admitted. 'A lot.'

'Good.' He traced the edge of her face with a fingertip. The feel of his skin gliding against hers made every nerve-ending fizz.

'Kiss me, Lorenzo,' she whispered.

He did.

Slowly. Taking his own sweet time about it and heating her blood to fever pitch until she forgot everything else except him.

He removed the sash, spun her round so her back was to him, scooped her hair over her shoulder to bare her nape to him, and then traced the edge of her dress with one fingertip. 'I like this, Indi,' he said. 'The softest velvet. Except your skin's even softer. Though I need to prove that theory. Empirical evidence is very important.' He undid the first button, then the next, and stroked every centimetre of skin as he uncovered it.

And then she felt his lips brushing her skin very lightly. She shivered. 'Lorenzo.'

'You're beautiful,' he said softly. 'And you smell of roses.'

She smiled. 'It's my favourite scent. I love the garden here in summer because it's like drinking roses when you breathe.'

'I'm going to think of you every time I smell roses,' he said, and traced a path with his mouth all the way down her spine.

Then he turned her to face him again, slid the dress off her shoulders, and scooped it up from the floor when she'd stepped out of it. To her amusement, he hung her dress neatly over the back of the rococo chair next to the matching dressing table. 'Details?' she asked. 'Or are you just a buttoned-up neat freak?'

'Details,' he said. 'Attention to them is…' His gaze heated. 'Essential.'

Meaning that he intended to pay very close attention to her? Her knees went weak at the thought.

'You're wearing too much,' she said, aware that she was only wearing skimpy, lacy underwear and the only thing out of place for him was his bow tie. 'I think we need to even this up slightly.'

'What do you suggest?' he asked.

The choice was too delicious. 'I'm not sure whether I want you to strip for me, or whether I want to undress you myself,' she confessed.

'I have a practical solution. Pick one,' he said, 'and you can do the other next time.'

There was definitely going to be a next time?

'Then right now I get to undress you,' she whispered. And she did it very slowly, helping him shrug out of his jacket and then enjoying discovering the texture of his skin as she unbuttoned his shirt. 'I've changed my mind about you being James Bond. I think you're Mr Darcy.'

'Are you suggesting skinny-dipping in the lake, Ms Moran?'

'No. It's like the director said—it's better when something's left to the imagination.' She smiled. 'But you in a

white shirt, rising out of the lake and looking all sexy—
yes, that would be very nice. Very nice indeed.'

'I'll see what I can do,' he promised. 'You'd make a rubbish valet, by the way.'

'How?'

'You're much too slow. I've lost patience.'

'Pulling rank, are we?' she teased. The king-to-be and
the commoner.

'Totally.' He kissed her, and swiftly finished stripping.
Then he placed his hands on her shoulders, holding her at
a distance so he could look his fill. 'Indigo Moran,' he said
huskily, 'you are totally luscious.' With that, he picked her
up and carried her over to the bed.

And after that neither of them spoke for a long, long
time.

CHAPTER FIVE

THE NEXT MORNING, Indigo woke, her head pillowed on Lorenzo's shoulder and his arms wrapped round her.

For a moment, she felt cherished and safe.

And then she shook herself. That wasn't the deal.

Even so, she couldn't help wondering: how long had it been since she'd woken like this, wrapped in a man's arms?

She really couldn't remember.

She'd dated men before Nigel, but she'd been more focused on her work than on relationships in art college. She'd wanted to prove to her grandparents that she'd done the right thing in rebelling against the education her father had planned, and that she wasn't flighty like her mother. She'd always put her studies first. And it had paid off, because she'd ended up with a first-class degree and a job working for a very prestigious glass studio.

Though Indigo hadn't been one for all work and no play. She'd attended plenty of parties, dated whoever she wanted to see, and when it had suited her she'd let things go further than a chaste kiss good-night at the door of her flat. But committing to a relationship, putting herself in a position where her heart could be broken—she'd avoided that as much as possible, keeping her relationships light and fun through college and most of her working life.

Until Nigel.

And that had been the biggest mistake of her life. She'd fallen in love with him and got her heart well and truly stomped on in the process. And, with Nigel, she'd never actually woken in his arms. He'd never stayed overnight in the six months they'd been together and he'd never invited her back to his place, saying that he lived and worked on the other side of London from her and the extra commute would be a nuisance for both of them.

Why had she never questioned that? Why had she just accepted it?

But there was no point in beating herself up about the past. Indigo knew she wasn't going to make the same mistake again. This time, she was protected against heartbreak. Right from the start she and Lorenzo had agreed that this was just a mad fling. One with a time limit. She wasn't going to fall in love with His Royal Highness Prince Lorenzo Torelli. This was going to be light and sweet and fun, a kind of respite for both of them. And she was going to enjoy every second of their fling.

It was still very early in the morning, and the summer sunlight was just seeping around the edges of the curtains. She shifted slightly so she could lie on her side and watch him sleeping.

In repose, Lorenzo was truly beautiful. He had a perfect bone structure and long, long lashes that made her itch to sketch him. And the way his mouth turned up at the corners naturally made it look as if he was smiling in his sleep. Or maybe he *was* smiling in his sleep. Dreaming of her, perhaps, and the way they'd made love in the ancient four-poster bed?

She smiled. Lorenzo had proved himself a spectacular lover, too. He'd paid attention to detail, noticed where she liked being touched and how she liked being kissed. The first time they'd made love should've been awkward and ever so slightly embarrassing, but it hadn't been that way. It had felt so natural, so right: unexpectedly and wonderfully perfect.

She couldn't resist leaning over and kissing his mouth, very lightly.

His eyes opened. She saw the second that he focused and realised where he was. And then he smiled. The kind of smile that could melt the most frozen heart.

'Good morning, Indi,' he said softly.

Her heart did a backflip. 'Good morning, Lorenzo.'

He moved slightly closer. 'Was that my imagination, or did you just kiss me awake?'

She wrinkled her nose. 'Sorry. I didn't mean to wake you. But you looked like Sleeping Beauty, and I'm afraid it was a bit too much to resist.'

He coughed. 'I hate to tell you this, Indi, but Sleeping Beauty was a girl. And I'm not a girl.'

No. He was all man. And the thought of how they'd made love last night, how his body had felt inside hers, sent a warm glow through her. 'Hey, there's no reason why a man can't be beautiful.' She spread her hands. 'I mean, "Sleeping Handsome" doesn't sound right, does it?'

'Is that how you see me?' he asked.

'Kind of yes and kind of no.' She thought about it. 'I like the idea of playing around with fairy tales, seeing what happens if you change an element.'

He looked at her and sighed. 'I have a nasty feeling I know where this is going. Please tell me you're not planning to do a series of stained-glass windows with all the fairy tale roles reversed—and with me as the model.'

'If things were different,' she said, 'I'd talk you into that, because it's a *brilliant* idea. But it's not going to happen,' she reassured him, stroking his hair back from his forehead. 'That's why I said yes, that's kind of how I see you—because you're from a different world. And being here with me is almost like a temporary enchantment. Except in this case it doesn't involve spinning wheels and pricking your finger, you're not going to sleep for a hundred years—oh, and a kiss isn't supposed to break the spell,' she added hastily.

'I'm glad to hear it.' He shifted so that he could pull her back into his arms. 'Well, now you've woken the sleeping prince, I think there's only one thing to do.'

And he kissed her until they were both dizzy.

'Now that's a way to start a morning,' she said with a smile.

He smiled back. 'My thoughts exactly. But I'd better go back to my own room before everyone else in the house wakes up. Do you always wake at the crack of dawn, Indi?'

'Not always, but I'm not actually that used to sharing my sleeping space,' she admitted.

He stroked her face. 'Good. Just for the record, neither am I.'

'Good.' She kissed him. 'Now disappear before you bump into Gus's mum, still wearing last night's clothes, and embarrass everyone.'

'Yes, ma'am,' he teased, and climbed out of bed. He gave her a sidelong glance. 'Shouldn't you be looking away while I get dressed?'

'My degree's in art. I've taken enough life drawing classes that I'm very comfortable with people being naked in front of me.' She raised an eyebrow. 'Has anyone told you that your posterior view is nicer than that of Michelangelo's David?'

To her delight, he actually blushed. 'No. But thank you for the compliment.' He finished dressing—though he left his shirt collar open and didn't bother with the bow tie—

then came to sit beside her on the bed. 'When will you be free today?'

'After the house and garden are closed, late this afternoon.' Much as she wanted to spend time with him, enjoy every precious second, she had commitments and it wouldn't be fair to back out. Though she knew he understood; he was busy, too, and they'd agreed to see each other in the spaces between each other's work.

'Maybe we could take a walk in the grounds when you're free.'

'I'd like that,' she said. 'Maybe I could text you when my workroom's clear, and you can text me back to let me know where and when to meet you.'

'Good idea.' He fished his mobile phone from his pocket. 'What's your number?'

She told him. A couple of moments later, her mobile beeped. She opened the text. 'A smile and a kiss. Works for me,' she said, smiling and kissing him. 'See you later, Lorenzo.'

She didn't see him at breakfast, because she ate a hasty bowl of granola, yoghurt and fruit in the kitchen rather than the breakfast room and she took her coffee through to her workroom. Lorenzo didn't come to see her while she was working on the glass in the morning; no doubt he had king-in-waiting stuff to do, she thought. And then the house opened for visitors, and she was busy talking to people and showing them what she was doing.

Once the last visitor had left, she sent a quick text to Lorenzo, letting him know that she was free.

See you in the rose garden in half an hour, was his reply.

When she walked into the rose garden, he was sitting on one of the wrought iron benches beneath a bower of roses. Again, she thought of the Sleeping Beauty story and how she'd love to paint Lorenzo in a stained-glass window. And she smiled when she realised that Toto, the elderly golden Labrador, was sitting patiently next to him, his chin on Lorenzo's knee.

'I hope you don't mind us having a companion. Toto rather insisted on coming along,' Lorenzo said wryly.

She laughed and made a fuss of the dog. 'No, it's nice having a dog around. Especially in a garden as gorgeous as this one.'

'Did you have a good day?' he asked.

She nodded. 'I made quite a lot of progress on the mermaid and had some interesting chats with the visitors. You?'

'I worked through some files for my grandfather.'

'And you need some downtime?' she guessed.

'Just a little,' he admitted.

She heeled off her shoes, and sighed in bliss as her feet sank into the soft lawn. 'Ah, that's better. The only thing I don't like about my job is that you need to wear shoes all the time.'

'In case of splinters?' he asked.

She nodded. 'And this is bliss. The softest grass in the world.'

The way she'd just pushed off her shoes and was walking barefoot on the lawn... Lorenzo envied the way that Indigo could just act on impulse. It was something he never did; he was always aware of the consequences of his actions. Which was a good thing, but it also meant that he missed out on the joy that Indigo seemed to find so easily in things. 'Don't you worry about getting a thorn in your feet?'

'Hardly. Roses drop petals rather than thorns,' she pointed out.

'Even so. Sometimes they drop branches.'

'Which I can see and avoid.' She laughed. 'Though I admit I wouldn't walk barefoot by the lake. The ducks are a bit indiscriminate about where they have a toilet break and it's annoying having to watch where you put your feet instead of being able to watch the water and the sky.' She looked at him. 'Why don't you take your shoes off?'

'What, now?'

'Yes, now. Feel the grass under your feet. It's cool and springy and lovely.'

When was the last time he'd walked barefoot on the grass? Probably not since he was a small child. But, not wanting to appear a total stick-in-the-mud, he complied. He tucked his socks into his shoes and let his shoes dangle from one hand, just as she was doing.

'You're right,' he said, when he'd taken a couple of steps on the cool, soft grass. 'It's wonderful.'

'When was the last time you walked barefoot on a beach?' she asked.

He shrugged. 'I really can't remember.'

'Is there some rule at prince school that you should always be fully, impeccably dressed unless you're in the shower?'

He knew she was teasing him, but at the same time she had a point. As a prince, he always had to look the part. Not that he was going to let himself dwell on that side of things. 'Or swimming,' he said lightly. 'Unless of course you're dressed in Regency costume and want to turn some heads. Then you're allowed to be partially undressed. Especially in a lake,' he added, knowing that it would amuse her.

She laughed, and he loved the way she tipped her head back, her face up towards the sunlight and her face full of smiles. 'You half promised me that before, Lorenzo. I am *so* holding you to that Mr Darcy moment.'

'Talking about holding...' He brushed his free hand against hers.

'Would that be a hint, Your Royal Highness?' she teased.

He rolled his eyes. 'Are you saying that I have to give you an official royal order?'

'No. I probably wouldn't obey an order. But I can take a hint.' She smiled again and twined her fingers through his.

Walking through the rose garden with her, hand in hand, with the dog pattering along beside them, felt like being in another world. An enchanted bubble. Maybe she was right when she said he reminded her of Sleeping Beauty, Lorenzo thought, because this was like a dream. It wasn't real. They couldn't have a future. He needed to find a future queen for Melvante, someone his grandfather and his political advisers would approve of—and they definitely wouldn't approve of Indigo, despite her charm and her work ethic. And he already knew that Indigo hated his world; she'd escaped it before and wouldn't want to go back.

So he was going to enjoy every second of their fling together and take it for what it was: a beautiful interlude, a few moments out of time.

'So why do you have a thing about roses?' he asked.

'They're beautiful, they smell nice, and they look stunning in a stained-glass window. They're probably the perfect flower,' she said.

He smiled. 'My grandfather would agree with you. He has a rose garden.'

'One he tends himself?'

'When he gets the chance, yes. I'll know exactly where to find him when he's retired.' Lorenzo was surprised by her perception. She'd clearly worked out that what music did for him, roses did for his grandfather. 'So do roses figure much in stained glass?'

'Quite a bit,' she said. 'I'm trying to talk Syb into letting me do a window of roses for the library. Well, I know technically Gus should make the final decision, but he wants it done as a birthday present for his mum and he says it's her choice.' She looked wistful. 'I'd love to make a window full of roses. I'd have one myself if I had the right house.'

'And your house isn't right?'

'It's a modern bijou flat. Rented.' She gave a half-shrug. 'I'm not there very much, so it doesn't make sense to have a large place. I'm either at my studio, or working on location somewhere.'

'I guess,' he said. But still he wondered, if what Indigo really wanted was to have roots? She'd grown up with her grandparents; deep down, did she want a space of her own?

'So what about you? I assume as the prince you have to live in the castle?'

'I have an apartment in the castle,' he said. 'I can be independent if I choose and cook my own meals.'

She smiled at him. 'As *if* a prince is going to cook for himself. I bet you have a team of chefs who pamper you to within a millimetre of your life.'

That was a little too close to home. When was the last time he'd cooked for himself? Normally, he was so busy that it was easier to eat something prepared by the castle chefs when he was in Melvante, and to get takeout if he was in London. 'I make an excellent chilli, I'll have you know,' he protested. 'I learned to cook when I was a student—and, actually, I like cooking.' He just didn't do it that often, any more.

She raised her eyebrows at him. 'Is that a cue for a challenge, Your Royal Highness?'

'Maybe.' He knew he'd enjoy cooking for her; he could imagine her sitting at his kitchen table in bare feet, chatting and maybe sketching as he cooked. Then he shook himself. Such domestic scenes weren't going to happen, however much he might like them to. She wasn't going to be in his apartment at the castle and he was hardly ever going to get the time to cook or play the piano. He definitely wasn't going to have much time to do ordinary things like this—walking hand in hand with a pretty girl in a rose garden.

He pushed the thought away.

As if she noticed that he'd gone quiet and brooding, and she wanted to change the subject to something that would be less painful for him, she asked, 'So what's your castle like?'

That was an easier topic to talk about. 'It's pretty much your standard picture-postcard European castle. White stone, lots of turrets with pointed tiled roofs, a drawbridge and a moat.'

'That sounds nice. What about inside?'

'Red carpets, oak panelling and suits of armour—and there's a gallery with pictures of every King of Melvante since Carlo the First.'

'Will you be the first Lorenzo?' she asked.

'The third—my grandfather's the second.' His father had been supposed to be the third, with himself as the fourth. How different his life would've been, had his father lived.

'So you were named after your grandfather?'

He nodded. 'How about you?'

She looked rueful. 'I think my mum just picked the most unusual name she could think of. And possibly something that would annoy my father, because it's not very traditional.'

He thought of the traditional royal English names. 'I can't see you as an Elizabeth, a Mary or an Anne.'

'Maybe if I'd been Elizabeth, I would've fitted in at

school. I could've been Lizzie in the four musketeers of our dorm,' she mused.

He shook his head. 'Even if you'd had an L in your name, you wouldn't have been part of those girls. Besides, if you'd really hated your name, you could've used your middle name. Or any other name you liked, for that matter.'

'I hated my name when I was really small—in the days when I needed to feel I fitted in,' she admitted, 'and back then some of the girls weren't very nice, saying it wasn't a proper name for a girl because it was a colour.'

'There are plenty of colours used as names. Ruby, Jade and Amber,' he said, taking the first three that came into his head.

'They're gemstones,' she corrected.

'How about Violet and Rose?'

She shook her head. 'Flowers.'

'Scarlet,' he said. 'Even you can't argue against *that* one.'

'I guess not.' She grinned. 'Nowadays, I like my name.'

'So,' he said, 'do I. It suits you and it suits your job.'

She gave him a half-bow. 'Why, thank you, Your Royal Highness. Anyway, before I sidetracked you, you were telling me about your art collection. Lots of portraits of kings.'

'My great-grandfather collected art. You'd like what he bought.' He smiled at her. 'And there's a picture of my great-great-grandmother you'd really love. She sat for Burne-Jones when she was a child.'

'How fantastic. I hope you know I'm horribly envious.'

'Maybe you can come and see it.' The offer was out before he could stop it.

'Maybe.' She gave him the sweetest, sweetest smile.

And he knew without having to ask that it was a polite way of saying no.

She paused. 'OK. You like the building and you like the art. But is it home?'

He thought about it. 'Yes, it is. I have a lot of happy memories there.' Despite his parents' early deaths, the lies he'd been told to spare him from the truth and the shock of discovering that his father had had such a dark side.

'I'm glad.' Her fingers tightened briefly round his. 'So what are you going to do when you're king?'

'Build on the work of my grandfather and make my people proud of me,' he said promptly.

'Good goals,' she said approvingly. 'How do you plan to get there?'

Lorenzo found himself talking seriously to Indigo about Melvante, about his people and what he wanted to do for his country. Whenever he stopped, thinking that maybe he was being too boring and ought to change the subject, she drew him out a little more, asking questions that showed she'd been paying attention to what he'd said and coming up with ideas that really made him think. And he was oddly pleased that she was showing as much of an interest in his job as he had in hers.

Toto flopped down with a grunt; she stopped, and made a fuss of the old dog. 'I think we've tired him out, poor old boy.' She glanced back at the house. 'Look how far we've walked. I don't think he's going to find the return walk very easy.'

'Then I'll carry him back.' Lorenzo put his shoes back on, preparing to pick up the dog. Toto was slightly overweight and a bit on the heavy side, but no way was Lorenzo going to abandon the old dog. He'd allowed Toto to join them for a walk and he hadn't thought enough of the fact that the dog was elderly now and couldn't walk as far as he'd been able to run alongside them when Lorenzo and Gus had been students and Toto had been a boisterous pup.

'Lorenzo, you ca–'

Her protest died as he picked up the dog.

'You're an elephant, Toto. You need to go on a doggy diet,' he informed the dog, who licked his nose gratefully.

When he glanced at Indigo, he was surprised to see a film of tears in her eyes. 'What's wrong, Indi?' he asked gently.

'You're going to be a king next month. And there you are, carrying an old dog home.'

'Toto and I go back a long way. And you always look after your own, don't you?' He smiled at her. 'Strictly speaking, he's Gus's dog. But I spent enough time here as a student to think of him as at least partly mine.'

'Even so. A lot of people would…' She swallowed hard. 'Well, just leave him.'

'Until he'd had a rest and could find his own way back to the house? No way.' He grimaced. 'I suppose we could've gone to find a wheelbarrow and a blanket for him, but I wouldn't abandon him just because he's old and tired and needs a break.'

'I guess.'

She was quiet until they got to the house, where he gently set Toto back on to his feet.

'You're a good man, Lorenzo Torelli,' she said softly. 'And you're going to make an awesome king.'

'I hope so,' he said, equally softly. 'I really hope so.'

CHAPTER SIX

OVER THE NEXT WEEK, Lorenzo and Indigo spent as much time together as they could, while trying to be discreet and not flaunt their affair in everyone's faces. Every sneaked moment was precious.

'I'm still thinking about how you carried Toto back to the house. He weighs a ton, and you carried him for ages. Do you do weight training or something?' Indigo asked when they were curled up on Lorenzo's bed together.

'Or something.'

'Which is?'

'Come and train with me in Gus's fitness room, and I'll show you,' Lorenzo said.

The fitness room? It was one of the rooms at Edensfield Indigo had never set foot in; she'd never been remotely interested in running on a treadmill or picking up weights. 'But I'm not sporty. I was always the last one picked for the team at lacrosse. And even when I moved to the local secondary school, I was never any good at netball, hockey or rounders. I used to get an A for effort and a D for achievement.'

'The trick is to find something that you enjoy doing.'

'I didn't enjoy team sports. At all,' she said with a grimace. 'I don't mind going for a long walk—I'm not a total couch potato—but I'm really not sporty.' She stroked his pectorals and his abs. 'You have muscles—a proper six-pack. So I guess that means you're really sporty.'

'Mens sana in corpore sano,' he intoned.

'A healthy mind in a healthy body,' she translated. 'More prince school stuff?'

He laughed. 'You translated it, so I thought you'd know where it comes from.'

'I only studied Latin to help me with the glass—sometimes you get wills or what have you to help you with the provenance of the glass. People donating particular windows to a church, that kind of thing.'

'It's Juvenal, from the *Satires*. And it doesn't just apply to princes—it's a list of what he thinks you should ask for in life. I can't remember the whole lot, but it includes a stout heart, one that's not scared of hard work and isn't angry or lustful...' He leaned over to kiss her. 'Most of that works for me. Except the lustful bit. Because you're incredibly desirable, Indigo Moran, and you make me feel lustful. Very lustful indeed.'

'Why, thank you, Your Royal Highness. I would curtsey in gratitude—'

'Would you, hell.' He stole another kiss.

'Let me finish. I would curtsey in gratitude for the compliment, but...' She laughed. 'Well, I'm comfortable and I don't want to move.'

'I don't want you to move, either.' He tightened his arms round her.

'So what sport do you do?' She thought for a moment. 'You promised me a Mr Darcy moment, so I'm guessing swimming.'

'I can swim, but it's not my favourite.'

'Rowing, then?' She looked at him. 'And I bet you got a Blue for it at Oxford.'

'Well, yes,' he admitted. 'But rowing isn't my favourite, either.'

She was intrigued. 'Tennis? Cricket? Rugby?'

'That's three more guesses—and all wrong. Forfeits are due,' he said, claiming a kiss for each.

'OK. I give up. Tell me.'

'Sparring.'

'*Boxing?* No way.' She shook her head. 'They'd never let a king-to-be take a risk like that. Boxing's dangerous. People get seriously hurt.'

'Sparring just means padwork. So I get all the fun of boxing but without the risk of being hurt,' he said. 'Come and spar with me.'

'I hate to point this out, Your Royal Highness, but you're six inches taller than I am and I'm not exactly muscle-bound. I'm not going to be a very good sparring partner, am I?'

'Sure you are. You'll work with the gloves, not the pads.'

'And I don't have any workout gear.'

'Borrow some from Lottie or Maisie. They're both about your size, so one of them is bound to have something she can lend you.'

He clearly wasn't going to let this go. 'So when are we doing this training, then?'

'Tomorrow morning. I was thinking the crack of dawn, given that you always seem to wake so early.'

It really wasn't her idea of fun, but she'd indulge him. 'OK.'

'Good.' He nuzzled the hollows of her collarbones. 'So, where were we?'

Later that day, Indigo borrowed a T-shirt and a pair of shorts from Lottie—at least she had a pair of training shoes with her—and the next morning she followed Lorenzo to the fitness room.

He handed her a skipping rope. 'This is a speed rope. It's weighted so you can skip properly.'

'Skipping?' She looked at him, mystified. 'I thought we were doing boxing stuff?'

'We are. This is to warm up your muscles.'

She managed five skips before she tripped over the rope.

'You need to jump over the rope with both feet together,' he explained, 'not one foot at a time as if you're a rocking horse.'

She spread her hands. 'That's the way I learned to skip at school.'

'This is boxing skipping. It's much more effective at getting your heart rate up and warming up your muscles.'

'What's the difference?'

'Watch.' He skipped slowly, jumping over the rope; then he quickened his pace and it was as if he were floating on air. His feet didn't even seem to touch the ground—he just seemed to be hovering mid-air.

'Now that's just showing off,' she grumbled, wanting to hide just how impressed she was.

He laughed. 'No, that's practice. Do a little bit every day and eventually you'll be able to do this.'

She didn't think so. 'Show me again.'

He coughed. 'You're trying to wriggle out of doing it.'

'All right.' She rolled her eyes. 'I admit that was seriously impressive, Your Royal Highness, and I'd like to see you do it again.'

He laughed. 'OK. I'll skip for you again. But you have to earn it.'

'That's mean,' she said.

'It's a carrot for a reward,' he corrected. 'If you want to see me skip, you have to do some skipping yourself, first. OK. Let's work on your technique.' He walked her over towards the mirror. 'Now, watch yourself in the mirror.'

'Haven't we just proved that I can't skip?'

'We've just proved that you panicked and you need to change your technique,' he corrected. 'Remember what I said: jump over the rope with both feet together, and watch your feet in the mirror. Focus on lifting your feet.'

She tried again, and this time managed a few more skips before she tripped over the rope and had to stop.

'See? You're getting better. Now do it again. Watch your feet in the mirror and focus on the rhythm. Jump, jump, jump.'

She was hot and breathless by the time he finally let her stop. 'This is vile. I'm all sweaty and disgusting.'

He just grinned and kissed the tip of her nose. 'Tut, Ms Moran. Didn't your teachers tell you that horses sweat, men perspire and ladies glow?'

She glowered at him. 'I'm not a lady.'

He brushed his mouth against hers. 'I beg to differ. You're all woman, Indigo Moran, and right now you look as sexy as hell.'

And how was she supposed to concentrate, when he was looking at her like *that*?

He took the skipping rope from her and put the gloves on her. 'Right—now you need to keep your knees soft, crouch slightly, and keep your hands up to guard your face.'

He talked her through doing a jab and a cross, then put his hands into two pads and held them up. 'OK, now jab the pad to your right, then punch the one on your left. Remember to keep the hand you're not using up by your face.'

She hit the pads as he directed. This was surreal: *she was throwing punches at a king-to-be*. Surely there had to be laws against this.

'Harder,' he said.

She shook her head. 'But I might hurt you, Lorenzo.'

He smiled. 'Indi, my sweet, you're not going to hurt me. I wouldn't get you to hold the pads for me because I'm used to this and I'd hit too hard for you, but this is new to you and I assure you that you won't hurt me, however hard you hit. Now punch.'

By the time he called a halt, Indigo was breathing hard—and she was full of exhilaration. 'That was amazing! I get why you love it.'

'It's a great cardio workout, plus it's good for your arms and your abs. We're going to stop now or you'll be really sore tomorrow—actually, you might be sore anyway.' He looked faintly guilty. 'Sorry. I was enjoying that and I probably should've stopped earlier.'

'It's fine. I enjoyed it, too, even though I thought I'd hate it,' she said. 'And if anyone told me that a king-to-be would love putting on a pair of boxing gloves...'

He kissed her lightly. 'I'm a man first, Indi. Remember that.'

And the heat in his gaze sent a shiver of pure lust all the way from the top of her spine down to her toes.

'So now what?' she asked, her voice ever so slightly shaky.

'Now,' he said, 'we go and shower.' He bent down so he could whisper in her ear, 'And my vote is for us to do that together.'

'No arguments from me,' she said, feeling breathless.

He took off the gloves, and kissed the back of her hand. 'You did really well.'

'Because you're a good teacher.' She smiled at him.

'So were you, when you talked me through cleaning the lead cames.'

'It's just a matter of being clear with your instructions, paying attention and adapting things to suit the person you're teaching.'

'It's the same with this,' he said, and kissed her again. 'Right. Shower. Now.'

'Yes, Your Royal Highness,' she said, and kissed him back.

The following morning, Lorenzo walked in to Indigo's workroom at half past eleven. 'Time for lunch.'

'Lunch?' She glanced at her watch. 'Isn't it a bit early?'

'No. It means we'll be finished before the house and grounds open at one.'

'Fair enough.' She made sure that all her electrical equipment was switched off and all the liquids were safely in sealed containers, and followed him out of the house.

He was carrying a wicker basket, she noticed. They found a nice spot on the lawn outside the hothouses with a view of the lake. Lorenzo produced a rug for them to sit on and shook it out. Then he spread out a red and white checked tablecloth next to the rug and set out plates, cutlery and two champagne flutes.

So much more stylish than the plastic box of food and slightly scuffed plastic cups she was used to on a picnic.

'So you talked someone in the kitchen into making all this for you?' she asked.

'Actually, no. I sent one of my team into the local town with a very specific list. And I put this together with my own fair hands.'

'Resourceful and able to delegate. Good combination,' she said. Though part of her wondered, did he ever yearn to be just an ordinary man who could nip out to the shops himself on the spur of the moment without it having to be planned like a military operation, complete with security detail, or having to send someone else out with his list?

The first box contained watercress, baby plum tomatoes, strips of yellow pepper and slices of mango. Then there was a box of sliced chicken, which he arranged on top. He added a pot of dressing. 'Creamy chilli and coconut. I forgot to ask if you liked spicy food,' he said.

'I do.'

He brought out some rich seeded bread, which he carved into chunks, and his next foray into the picnic hamper was for a pot containing a red purée. She sniffed as he took the lid off. 'It smells like strawberries.'

'Pureéd,' he said, and deftly put some in each champagne flute, which he topped off from a tiny bottle of champagne. 'I thought we'd have just enough for one glass each, so it won't make you drowsy or affect your work,' he said.

She took a sip. 'This is fabulous—what is it, a kind of strawberry Bellini?'

'Yes. It's called a Rossini.'

'Where did you discover these?'

He laughed. 'Elementary class at prince school?'

'Yeah, yeah.' She raised her glass in a toast to him. 'To you. And thank you so much for spoiling me so delightfully.'

'My pleasure.' He leaned over and kissed her lightly.

Indigo enjoyed the food and the sunshine; and she especially enjoyed the company.

When they'd finished the salad, Lorenzo fed her more strawberries and miniature macaroons the colour of pistachio that tasted of coconut.

'They're perfect,' she said blissfully.

He smiled. 'We aim to please.' He reached over and kissed the corner of her mouth. 'Crumb,' he said.

Two could play at that game, she thought, amused. She kissed the corner of his mouth. 'Smear of sugar.'

He just laughed, and kissed her until she was dizzy.

Finally, he settled back with his head in her lap, looking pensive. She stroked his hair away from his forehead. 'What are you thinking?'

'Sometimes I wish I could keep a moment in time,' he said.

'You can. In here.' She rested one hand over his heart. 'And in here.' She stroked his forehead.

'I'd keep this moment,' he said softly. 'A perfect English summer afternoon.'

She knew exactly what he meant. Sunshine glinting on the lake, birds singing, the scent of roses, strawberries and champagne… There was really only one thing missing. She reached over to pick some daisies.

'What are you doing?' he asked.

'Nothing. Just close your eyes and chill out,' she said, and proceeded to make a daisy chain. When she'd finished, she made it into a crown. 'For you,' she said, and he opened his eyes to see the crown just before she draped it over his head.

He looked unutterably sad for a moment, as if she'd just reminded him that he'd be wearing a much heavier crown in a few short weeks.

'Actually, I was thinking Oberon,' she said softly.

'"Ill met by moonlight, proud Titania"?'

'I hope we're not ill met.' She smiled at him. 'Trust you to know Shakespeare—or was your degree in English?'

'Economics. But I had friends who read English.'

'Did you not think about studying music?' she asked. Surely that had been the subject of his heart?

He shrugged. 'Economics was more practical.'

'But if you'd had a choice?'

'Then, yes, I probably would've studied music,' he admitted.

'I was lucky,' she said softly. 'I got to do what I love.'

'I love what I'm going to do,' he said, though his words

sounded a little hollow to her, and just for a second he looked so very, very lonely.

The only way she could think of to make it better was to kiss him.

His arms tightened around her as if he really needed her. When he broke the kiss, he said, 'I guess we'd better get back.'

She helped him clear away the picnic. 'Thank you for spoiling me, Lorenzo. I really enjoyed this.'

'My pleasure.' He stroked her face. 'I'm glad I could share it with you.'

And she was glad, too.

Later in the week, Indigo woke to find herself alone.

Lorenzo hadn't said anything to her about needing an early start or going up to London.

Or had he changed his mind about their fling?

Hurt, she got up and slipped her dressing gown on. Then she saw a note next to the bed. A 'Dear Jane' letter? she wondered.

Well, they'd agreed it was a fling. The fact that she was falling for him—more fool her.

Steeling herself, she picked up the note and read it.

Meet you at the lake, by the boathouse.

Not a 'Dear Jane' letter, then. He'd clearly left the note on his pillow and it had fallen off. And they'd had those conversations about Mr Darcy. Was he really going to do that? Or was he doing something crazy and spontaneous, like planning to row her across the lake to watch the sunrise?

She smiled, dressed swiftly and headed out to the lake.

Lorenzo was sitting there on the steps of the boat-house, wearing full Regency dress—including knee-length leather boots. He looked utterly fantastic and her heart did a backflip.

He sketched a salute to her as she neared him, then took off his boots.

She stopped. Was he really going to do what she thought he was about to do?

She watched as he shed his dark jacket, his cravat and finally his silk waistcoat, leaving them on the steps of the boathouse. And then he gave her the most sensual smile ever and dived into the lake, still wearing the cream-coloured breeches and loose white shirt.

'Oh, my God,' she said softly. 'Mr Darcy in the flesh.'

She watched him swim, his arms moving powerfully through the water. And then he emerged from the lake, the white cotton of his shirt plastered to his skin.

It was the sexiest thing she'd ever seen.

'Did I get it right?' he asked as she walked over to join him.

'Oh, yeah, you got it right.' And how embarrassing was it that her voice had practically dropped an octave, going all husky? 'And your hair goes slightly curly when it's wet. I never really noticed that before—and you've got those lovely huge dark eyes, just like Colin Firth...'

Lorenzo gave her a pained look. 'Oh, please. Don't go all fan-girly on me.'

'Hey, you ask Lottie—she'll say the same,' she protested. 'Mind you, I'm sure I read somewhere that Jane Austen based Mr Darcy on Byron.'

'I'm not sure about that. But even so I'm not mad, bad or dangerous to know,' he said.

She laughed and thought, actually, you are dangerous to know, because I could so easily fall in love with you, and that would be the most stupid thing ever—because I wouldn't fit into your world and you couldn't leave yours and join mine. Instead, she said more prosaically, 'I hope you brought some dry clothes.'

'Of course. Just as well, actually, because the lake was a bit colder than I thought it was going to be.' He took her hand and led her into the boating house, then stripped off and towelled himself dry.

'I'm pretty sure Mr Darcy didn't have a spare set of clothes nearby,' she commented, hoping that he couldn't hear how hard her heart was beating.

'But I didn't want to meet you in the garden and make small talk. Or drip water all over the carpets at Edensfield. Besides, Darcy would've needed a valet,' he pointed out.

She grinned. 'I would offer, but I've been told I'm a rubbish valet.'

He gave her a smouldering look. 'This could be your chance to prove me wrong.'

'I'd rather sketch you than dress you.'

He groaned. 'Don't tell me you've got pencils and a sketchpad with you.'

'No. But I do have this.' She tapped her head.

'You're wired with a hidden camera? Female James Bond, so there's a microphone in your lipstick and a camera in your contact lenses?'

'Very funny. You know what I meant.' Her memory.

And that was what they were doing, wasn't it? Making the most of their fling and making wonderful memories in their brief time together. Memories that were going a long, long way to wiping out some of the heartache Nigel had caused her.

He kissed her lingeringly. 'Come on. I need a hot shower. Preferably with you.'

'If that's a royal order,' she said with a grin, 'then it's one I'm quite happy to obey.'

'Good.'

This time, when he undressed her, he just let everything

drop to the floor in a crumpled heap—so different from the way he'd hung her velvet dress so neatly over the chair.

She laughed and kissed him. 'I'm glad you're losing your neat-freak ways.'

'You've taught me that spontaneous can be good,' he said.

She loved the fact that he was trying. For her. 'Planning can be good, too,' she said. It had definitely taken planning to sort out the picnic and that Mr Darcy moment, and she'd loved every second of them.

'Indi, you talk too much,' Lorenzo said, and proceeded to kiss her.

CHAPTER SEVEN

'ARE YOU BUSY tomorrow morning?' Indigo asked Lorenzo on the Friday morning.

He shrugged. 'I can move things if you want to do something.'

'Some of my favourite bits of glass in the country aren't very far from here. I thought I could take you to see them.'

He looked thoughtful. 'I'd like that. Bruno can drive us.'

'In your official car?' She hadn't really considered it before, but of course Lorenzo probably didn't drive himself very often. He couldn't go out without his security team being nearby, so everything he did had to be planned. 'But if people see a big black car in the car park, they'll immediately think there's a celeb in the church and rush in to see who it is. If they see my slightly battered van with "I Moran, Glass Restoration" on the side, they'll guess we're there to see the glass, so we won't be interrupted.'

'Is there room for my security team to sit in your van?' he asked.

She shook her head. 'There aren't any seats in the back—it's where I keep my tools or transport frames.'

'Much as I'd like to go—and I know your intentions are good,' he said softly, 'it wouldn't be fair on you or on my grandfather to leave here without my security team.'

'Sorry. I didn't think it through.' Whereas Lorenzo was

used to having to plan everything with military precision. And how awful it must be for him, she thought, never being able to do things on impulse and always having people watching his back. When did he ever get space just to *be*?

He leaned forward and kissed her lightly. 'We could compromise. There's always a way.'

Was there? She wasn't so sure.

'Your van isn't suitable and neither's my car. But maybe we can borrow a car from Gus that's a little more subtle. Bruno can drive us, and he and Sergio will give us space in the church to look around.'

'I'd like that,' she said.

'Good.' He kissed her lightly. 'I'll go and see Gus.'

'She's talked you into doing glass geek stuff with her?' Gus laughed. 'Lottie's going to be most put out at missing coffee and pastries.'

'I'll grovel and I'll promise to bring back some pastries for her,' Lorenzo said, laughing back.

'Of course you can borrow a car, idiot. Indi's right— if you take that huge black monster of yours, everyone's going to know there's a celeb about.'

'I'm not a *celeb*,' Lorenzo said, his voice pained.

'You are, where the papers are concerned.' Gus paused. 'This thing between you and Indi—are you sure it's a good idea?'

Lorenzo felt the colour seep into his face. 'We know what we're doing. It's temporary.'

'You've got the same look on your face as I'm sure there was on mine when I met Maisie,' Gus pointed out. 'And I've never seen you like this before.'

'It's temporary,' Lorenzo repeated. 'We'll both walk away when I go back to Melvante. And we'll part as friends.'

Gus raised an eyebrow. 'She's a lot more vulnerable

than she makes out, you know. If you hurt her, Lottie will fillet you.' He paused. 'Actually, no, I'll be first in line to call you out and I'll fillet you myself.'

'I'm not going to hurt her.' Lorenzo placed his hand briefly on Gus's shoulder. 'Though I'm glad she has some-one to look out for her.'

'She's had a rough deal where her family's concerned.'

'I know. She told me.'

'She told you?' Gus looked surprised. 'Then it's worse than I thought. She never talks about her family.'

'I'm not going to hurt her,' Lorenzo repeated.

'This is going to end in tears,' Gus warned, shaking his head.

'No, it's not. I'll make sure of that,' Lorenzo said.

Though he thought about Gus's words all afternoon. His best friend had fallen for Maisie and married her within six months. Two years later, they were still deliriously happy.

But the difference was, Gus and Maisie came from the same world. He and Indigo didn't. Well, they'd both been born to noble fathers, but that was as far as it went. Indigo had escaped from that world as soon as she possibly could, and no way would she ever go back to it. And she loved her job; she wouldn't be prepared to give that up for what she'd see as life in a goldfish bowl.

He shook himself. He wasn't in love with Indigo Moran, and she wasn't in love with him. They weren't planning a happy-ever-after. They were having fun and enjoying each other's company—taking a moment out of their usual lives. Gus was just seeing things through the rosy-tinted glasses of a happy marriage and impending fatherhood. Everything was going to be just fine.

On Saturday morning, Lorenzo breakfasted quickly with Indigo in the kitchen, then met his security team as arranged next to the car Gus was lending them. Bruno tapped the details of the church into the satnav system and drove them through narrow country lanes into a pretty little village. The flint-built church was set high on a mound at the edge of the village and, as Indigo had predicted, when Lorenzo twisted the huge iron ring in the heavy oak door the latch clicked up and allowed him to push the door open and follow her inside.

The church was beautiful; with two storeys of windows, it was full of light.

'Come and see my centaur. He's my favourite piece of glass in the world,' she said, and drew him over to one of the windows.

There was a circle of glass set into the diamond-paned window. The outside of the circle had a thick border of purple glass, and in the middle was a black and white picture highlighted with bright yellow, of a centaur playing a violin with a little dog running round his feet.

'And then there's this.' She turned him round and pointed at an angel.

He smiled. 'Trust you.'

'OK, so I have a thing for angels.' She smiled back. 'I just love Gabriel's feathery trousers. Did you know that when they did the medieval Mystery Plays, this is the sort of costume the angels wore?'

Her love for her subject was infectious as well as endearing. He loved her enthusiasm, and the fact that she had the scholarly information to back it up.

Just then, a woman walked in carrying an armful of flowers. She smiled at them. 'Oh, sorry, don't mind me. I'm just sorting out the flowers. We have a wedding here this afternoon,' she confided.

Lorenzo and Indigo exchanged a glance.

Weddings.

For one crazy moment, Lorenzo could imagine standing there in front of the altar, the church filled with roses and crammed with people wanting to share the moment, waiting for Indigo to walk down the aisle towards him.

Oh, help. Maybe Gus had had a point, because Lorenzo had never, ever visualised something like that before. He hadn't even thought about his future wedding, knowing that it would be more or less an arranged marriage for diplomatic purposes because the needs of his country had to come before his personal desires.

But, now the idea was in his head, he couldn't shift it: Indigo in a wedding dress and a veil, carrying a simple bouquet, walking down the carpeted aisle towards him.

'This would be the perfect place to get married,' Indigo said softly.

Was she thinking it, too? Imagining herself walking down the aisle…towards him?

As they moved away from the woman arranging the flowers, he couldn't help asking, 'Is this where you want to get married?'

'I'm never getting married.' She lifted her chin. 'Marriage is just a piece of paper, and it doesn't stop people lying or cheating.'

The hurt was obvious in her voice. Was she thinking about her parents' situation, he wondered, or had she been married before and been hurt by someone who'd cheated on her?

Her face twisted. 'Besides, marriage is an institution and I'm not very good at institutions.'

How he wanted to hold her. Tell her that everything would be OK and he'd never let anything hurt her again.

But it was a promise he knew he wouldn't be able to keep. Short of keeping Indigo wrapped in cotton wool, he couldn't guarantee to protect her from everything. And if she was wrapped in cotton wool, she'd lose her freedom. She'd suffocate. Just as his mother had.

How could he turn this round?

'If you ever did change your mind and get married, I bet it would be in a church with amazing glass,' he said. 'And I bet you'd have a really untraditional wedding dress and outrageous shoes.'

She smiled. 'I'd get my friend Sally to design it for me—the one who made the indigo dress. But I'm not getting married.' She took a deep breath. 'And you'll get married to someone wearing a specially made, hugely elegant and very traditional dress with lots of handmade lace. In a cathedral.'

'I guess.' Let it go, he told himself. *Let it go.* But his mouth had other ideas. 'You'd like the cathedral in Melvante. It's very gothic.'

'Good glass?'

'You'd be a better judge of that than I would.' He paused. 'Come and see for yourself.'

She shook her head, looking sad. 'We both know that when you go back, we won't see each other again. So let's not talk about this. We were talking about cathedrals.' She smiled. 'I love the cathedral in Norwich. There's a Burne-Jones window there and it's absolutely beautiful. I remember going Christmas shopping with Lottie one year, and we went to the carol service at the cathedral. There was a huge Christmas tree and lots of candles. It was totally magical, with the scent of the tree, the singing of the choir and the glass. We went to a patisserie afterwards, and it was just starting to snow, making it feel even more Christmassy. We had hot chocolate and the nicest coffee cake I've ever tasted.'

'Maybe we could go there now,' he suggested.

She shook her head. 'We're taking enough of a risk visiting a tiny country church. Bruno and Sergio would definitely not be happy with an unscheduled visit to the city.'

'I guess,' he said.

She looked at him and thought, there were so many things he couldn't do. She was so lucky to have her freedom and not be in his world.

She put some money in the church collection box; then they said goodbye to the flower-arranger and headed back outside into the bright sunlight.

'We need to go to the patisserie on the way back,' he said.

'Why?'

'Because I owe Lottie nice pastries. For coming out here with you in her place,' he explained.

She looked at Sergio. 'Are we allowed to visit a patisserie? Or maybe if I go in while His Royal Highness waits here in the car with you and Bruno?'

Lorenzo coughed. 'My life's not *that* restricted.'

Oh, yes, it was, she thought.

'We can all go to the patisserie, if His Royal Highness wishes,' Sergio said.

Indigo smiled. 'So I get to have morning coffee with three handsome men? Cool. That works for me.' She nudged Lorenzo. 'And would I be right in thinking that, being royal, you're like the Queen and you don't carry money, so this will be my treat?'

'No, you would not.' He looked offended. 'I can pay for coffee.'

She smiled. 'I was teasing. And offering. I'd like to buy you a coffee. Especially as you spoiled me with that picnic.'

'I'll pay,' Lorenzo said.

'You're not listening. I'm independent, Lorenzo. I've paid my own way since I got my first Saturday job at the age of fourteen. And I want to buy you coffee. I'd like to do something nice for you. So just shut up and let me do it, OK?'

* * *

For a moment, Lorenzo wondered if her ex had tried to take away her independence. Was that why she guarded it so very fiercely now?

He took her hand and squeezed it. 'Then thank you. Coffee would be very nice.'

The patisserie was crowded, but nobody seemed to pay much attention to the four newcomers. They were just part of the crowd. How long had it been since he'd managed that? he wondered.

Indigo ordered coffee and pastries for four, and Lorenzo was surprised to discover that the coffee was every bit as good as what he was used to in Melvante, and the pastries were delicate and delicious. And all the time, she chatted easily to Bruno and Sergio. He'd never known them so talkative, ever, even if one of them was training with him or sparring in the gym. Indigo had a gift for drawing people out. She could teach him so much. But what could he offer her, in return?

Indigo bought a box of treats for Gus, Lottie, Syb and Maisie before they left. And then she noticed a box of home-baked dog treats on the counter, so she bought some for all the dogs, too.

Lorenzo went quiet on the way back to Edensfield, but he held her hand all the way. And Indigo was aware that she was getting way too close to him. If this carried on, she'd get hurt. She really had to keep her heart protected and remember who he was. He could be her Mr Right Now, but not her Prince Happy-Ever-After. Much as she'd like him to be.

CHAPTER EIGHT

LORENZO'S LAST WEEK at Edensfield was idyllic. By day, he worked on official court business; his nights were spent making love with Indigo and sleeping with her wrapped in his arms; and in the spaces between they found time to go for long walks, hand in hand, or he'd play the piano for her, or she'd read to him with his head resting in her lap. Sometimes they watched the sun set over the lake; sometimes they lay on the damp grass and watched the stars. All the sweet, simple things that lovers did.

And he actually found himself writing music again— something he hadn't done in a long, long time. He knew he'd been inspired by Indigo and the way she acted on impulse and saw joy in everything.

Each day grew more bittersweet, because each day was nearer to the moment when he'd have to leave her.

And then it hit him.

He didn't want to leave her. He liked having Indigo in his life, and he was pretty sure she liked having him in her life. OK, so they'd agreed this would be a fling and it would end when he left for Melvante. But there was no reason why they couldn't renegotiate that agreement.

'Indi—I've been thinking,' he said, when they were lying on a blanket by the summer house, looking up at the stars.

'Should I be worried?' she teased.

'I leave in three days.'

'I know.' She stroked his face. 'I'll miss you.'

'I'll miss you, too.' He shifted so that he was facing her and could look into her eyes. 'That's why I've been thinking. It doesn't have to be like this.'

'Yes, it does. You're going off to be King of Melvante, and I'm staying here at Edensfield to finish my work on the library windows.'

'You've made a business commitment, and of course you want to honour that. But when you've finished here, there's nothing to stop you coming to Melvante and being with me.' He stole a kiss. 'Between-times, we're going to have to be pretty much long-distance, but we're only a couple of hours apart by plane. We can work something out.'

'Hang on. Are you saying you want to make this thing between us…?' She looked at him, wide-eyed.

'Official and no longer temporary. Yes.'

He wanted to be with her. In public as well as in private. And she wouldn't be Indigo Moran, stained-glass restorer, any more. She'd be the equivalent of a royal WAG, living her life on a public stage, hobbled by rules and regulations.

Yes, she'd be with Lorenzo. She wouldn't have to give him up.

But the misery of his lifestyle would eat into their relationship, sucking up all the love and leaving nothing but emptiness and hurt.

And she really, really didn't want that. She wanted to keep these memories intact. Perfect.

'Indi?' he asked.

Telling him the truth would hurt him. But going along with what he wanted would hurt him more, in the end. 'No, we couldn't,' she said softly. 'I wouldn't fit into your world, Lorenzo.'

'How do you know?'

'I just do.'

Which gave him nothing to argue against. He needed to know why she was so set against it. So he asked her straight out. 'Indi, what's so bad about my world?'

'It's full of rules and regulations. You're stuck in a box and you're expected to stay there. And you have to watch what you do, the whole time. Especially now there's social media—it means you can never switch off. You're being watched every second of the day. One accidental slip, and suddenly you've told the whole world something that maybe you would rather have kept private. It's like talking with a megaphone in the middle of a plinth on Trafalgar Square. And it gets passed on within seconds—juicy gossip.' She shuddered.

'And then someone else does something, and what you said or did is forgotten about.'

'Until the next time. Then it's dragged up again. Every little mistake is catalogued and held against you.'

'You'd be in a different position, as my partner,' he said. 'Nobody would try to put you down.'

She could see in his expression that he really believed it. For someone so clever, she thought, sometimes he just didn't have a clue what it was like in the real world. 'Maybe not to my face, but behind my back they would. Everyone expects you to marry a princess. And the press would be merciless. They'd want to know what you see in me. They'd dig up all the stuff about my parents.' And about Nigel—and she really didn't want to tell Lorenzo about that. She was too ashamed of how naive and stupid she'd been, having a relationship with a man who'd turned out to be married. And it still hurt to think about the miscarriage; talking about it was next to impossible.

'You can't be held to ransom by the choices your parents made,' he said.

'I can't fit into your world, Lorenzo. Don't ask me. I don't want to be the stick that the press uses to beat you. And we only have a few days left together. Please don't spoil it.'

What could he say to that?

All he could do was hold her.

And, that night, his lovemaking was much more intense. Yearning. If only she'd give them a chance, he was sure they could make it work.

But stubborn was definitely her middle name, and he didn't have a clue where to start convincing her that life with him wouldn't be anywhere near as scary as she feared.

On Lorenzo's last night, he fell asleep in Indigo's arms. She lay there, unable to sleep and wishing that she could somehow freeze time.

He'd asked her to make their relationship permanent. But how could she? She'd expose him to the kind of scandal he really didn't need, especially as he was just going to start ruling Melvante. She didn't want that tarnished.

'You're going to be a brilliant king,' she whispered, holding him close. 'Go with my love, always, and I wish things could've been different.'

Now, she knew she was always going to be on her own, because Lorenzo had spoiled her for other men. Nobody would ever match up to him, and it wouldn't be fair to get involved with someone else, knowing that he'd always be second best to Lorenzo. But being single was fine. She had good friends and her job. They'd see her through.

Though, when Lorenzo did marry his suitable princess, Indigo definitely wasn't going to tune in to the televised broadcast. She'd wish him luck, but she couldn't watch him marry someone else.

'I wish we'd met in another life,' she said softly. 'When things could have worked. But it wasn't to be, and we're going to be grown up about it. We're going to shake hands, say goodbye, and walk away from each other with our hearts intact.'

Even though she knew she was lying to herself.

When Lorenzo woke, the next morning, Indigo was still asleep. Her mermaid hair was spread all over the pillow, and her eyelashes were so long. So cute.

'If only you weren't so stubborn,' he said softly. Why couldn't she see that they could make it work? This was the twenty-first century, and a lot of the old social taboos had been broken. It didn't matter that she wasn't a princess. It didn't matter that her parents hadn't been married and that she was the child of an affair—it wasn't her fault. And he knew that Indigo was strong enough to hold her own in any social situation; she had a genuine warmth and enthusiasm that would draw people to her. Even those who maybe wouldn't want to accept her at first would come round, once they'd met her.

But the main stumbling block was Indigo herself.

If she didn't believe in herself—in their relationship—then it couldn't work.

How could he get her to believe?

He held her until she woke, then made love to her one last time. And he knew his own eyelashes were as wet as hers.

'We don't have to say goodbye,' he said, holding her close. 'We can make this work.'

She simply shook her head, as if not trusting herself to speak.

He sighed, and reached for his wallet. 'Here.'

She looked at the storage card. 'What's this?'

'For you. I wrote a song. Well, there aren't any words. But it's called "Indigo".'

'You wrote a song for me?'

'About how you make me feel.'

'Nobody's ever written a song for me before.' She stared at him in wonder. 'Thank you.'

'You might hate it.'

'I won't.'

Funny how she could be so sure of that, and yet she didn't have that same belief in *them*.

'Actually, I have something for you.' She slid out of bed and rummaged in a drawer, then handed him a cardboard tube. 'Don't look at it now. Later.'

She'd drawn something for him?

'Thank you,' he said softly.

She swallowed hard. 'I guess this is goodbye. I don't… not in front of everyone else.'

She'd be working when he left, he guessed. So she could hide behind her glass.

'I know,' he said softly. 'I'm not going to say the words.'

'Be happy,' she said. 'And you're going to be an awesome king.'

There was a lump in his throat and it was hard to get the words out. 'You be happy, too. And I hope you find someone who can give you what I can't.' Freedom. But he was pretty sure that she wouldn't find someone who loved her the way he'd grown to love her.

Later, on the plane back to Melvante, he opened the cardboard tube and took out the piece of cartridge paper. She'd drawn an angel in a rose bower—and the angel had his face.

Indigo and her angels. He smiled fondly, remembering

the church they'd visited together and the joy in her face as she'd shown him the glass.

Then he looked closer. Was it his imagination, or were those roses covering the bars of a cage?

That was how she saw his life. Trapped in a cage.

But it didn't have to be that way. It could be just roses. Somehow, he was going to have to convince her. And not just her: he also had to convince his grandfather that he'd found the woman who would be right for him and right for Melvante.

And maybe a little space between them—space where she had time to think and time to miss him—would help him do that.

CHAPTER NINE

THE BED WAS too wide, the days were too long and everything felt muted.

So much for being able to walk away intact at the end of their affair, Indigo thought. She'd really been deluding herself.

Still. Lorenzo had gone back to Melvante, where he belonged, and that was that. She still had the job she loved, and some good friends who were every bit as good as family. So she'd be just fine, she told herself sternly. Crying herself to sleep was pointless and ridiculous.

But she found it really hard to face breakfast in the mornings.

And she kept waking up at night. Which was ridiculous. At her age, she shouldn't need to get up in the middle of the night to go to the loo.

And maybe it was time she started watching what she ate, because her bra was feeling too tight.

A nasty, insidious thought wormed its way into her brain. Wonky appetite, tight bra, needing the loo in the middle of the night…She'd been there before, a couple of years ago. When her life had imploded.

No. Of course not. She was being paranoid. She and Lorenzo had always been careful about contraception. The last thing a king-to-be needed was an accidental baby, particularly when there was no way he could marry the baby's mother. And she had seriously unhappy memories from her miscarriage, two years ago.

But, now she thought about it, her period *was* a few days late. And she was usually regular down to the hour.

Maybe her period was late because she was stressed and upset about Lorenzo leaving. She hoped so. Because the alternative—that somehow their contraception had failed—would make life way, way too complicated.

Toto had taken to following Indigo about since Lorenzo had left, and tended to stay by her side in the workroom. The Labrador thumped his tail against the floor and nuzzled her knee, as if to say that he could tell she was upset and he was there.

'Lovely boy.' Indigo bent to make a fuss of him. 'I'm being stupid. Of course I'm not pregnant. I can't be.'

Though being pregnant would also explain why she kept crying. The tears could be due to her hormones running amok, not just because she missed the man she loved but knew she couldn't have.

'I can't be pregnant,' she said again.

Though she knew she wouldn't be able to settle until she knew the truth.

After the visitors had left Edensfield and her workroom was silent again, she drove to the nearest large town where she knew she'd be anonymous and bought a pregnancy test from the supermarket.

'Indigo Moran, you're being totally ridiculous. Of course you're not pregnant, and this is going to prove it once and for all,' she told herself sternly.

Back in her bathroom at Edensfield, she did the test, and watched the windows. One to show that she'd performed the test properly, and one that could turn her life upside down.

The last time she'd done a pregnancy test, she'd cried with joy, thinking that although the baby wasn't planned it would give Nigel the excuse he needed to commit properly to her. That she'd have their baby. That once again in her life she'd have someone who was related to her by blood, someone she could love and who'd love her back.

Nigel's reaction to the news had shocked her to the core. But she'd decided to keep the baby; after all, it wasn't the baby's fault that its father had turned out to be a cheat and a liar.

And then, six weeks later, she'd felt the drag low in her belly as she'd miscarried.

She sucked in a breath. This wasn't going to be like that. At all. Because she wasn't pregnant. She wasn't. She couldn't be.

Shaking herself mentally, she glanced at the test stick again.

And then she saw the result.

Positive.

Melvante might be his home, but it wasn't where his heart was, Lorenzo thought.

Being without Indigo for the last few days had crystallised for him exactly what he wanted in a life partner— someone who was bright and sparkly in her own right, who would support him and help him think straight by asking awkward questions, and who would keep her own interests in life, too. He loved her free-spiritedness.

Except he knew she was right about the sticking point. She'd hate what his lifestyle would become, once he was crowned king.

But there had to be a middle way. There had to be space for compromise. And hopefully, if she missed him as much as he missed her, she'd help him work out a compromise to suit them both.

He lasted two more days before he tackled his grandfather at the breakfast table.

'Nonno, you know you said I should think about marriage?'

'Yes.' His grandfather poured them both more coffee. 'So you're ready to discuss it? Good. I've drawn up a list of suitable brides.' He smiled at Lorenzo. 'Just as my father did for me.'

'That's the point, Nonno. I've already met the woman I want to marry,' Lorenzo said. 'Her name's Indigo Moran, she's a stained-glass restoration specialist, and she's—well, she makes me a better man. And I know I'll be a better king if I marry for love rather than duty.'

'I've had this conversation before.' His grandfather grimaced. 'With your father. He married for love, and look what happened.'

He'd ended up driving his car into a brick wall, with Lorenzo's mother by his side, killing them both. The rest of the world thought it was a tragic accident, but Lorenzo and his grandfather knew the truth: it had been a deliberate act, because Lorenzo's father couldn't bear the idea of his wife leaving him.

Lorenzo looked his grandfather straight in the eye. 'Nonno, I've spent most of my life trying to show you that I'm not my father. Indigo is nothing like my mother.'

'Your father married for love and it went wrong,' his grandfather pointed out. 'I married for duty, and your grandmother and I were happy together. We both knew what was expected of us.'

'I want to marry someone who understands my work and supports me,' Lorenzo said.

'Which your grandmother did for me.'

'Did you love Nonna?' Lorenzo asked.

'I respected her and I admired her,' his grandfather said. 'So, yes, I loved her.'

'Whenever you saw her, did your heart beat faster and the world seem a little brighter?'

His grandfather smiled ruefully. 'Lorenzo, you're confusing passion with love. Love is something that grows out of respect and mutual understanding. Something solid. Passion…that never lasts. It's like a firework—it burns brightly, it feels spectacular, and it's over almost immediately. Take my advice, and marry for sense—don't marry for passion. Your father married for passion, and he regretted it.'

'I'm not my father,' Lorenzo said again. 'I was thinking—you wanted to do something to mark the coronation. We could commission a rose window for the castle.'

'And you just *happen* to know a glass specialist,' his grandfather said wryly.

Lorenzo smiled. 'OK, so that was a little unsubtle. But it's a good way for you to meet Indi without raising any expectations on either side.'

'How does she feel about you?' his grandfather asked.

'That's tricky,' Lorenzo said. 'She has doubts about the world we live in. She thinks it's like a goldfish bowl.'

'It is, and she's right to have doubts. Our world isn't an easy one.' His grandfather sighed. 'You need to understand that you and I have responsibilities that other people don't. We have to put the needs of our country before our own needs. Which is why you need to marry someone who can cope with our world. Someone who's been brought up in it. Someone who doesn't have doubts.'

'Just meet her,' Lorenzo said. 'Give her a chance. And maybe she can give our world a chance.'

'And then?'

'We'll play it by ear,' Lorenzo said decisively.

'You've changed,' his grandfather said. 'The Lorenzo I know plans everything a long way in advance.'

Which was how he'd been brought up. Formal and rigid and disconnected from people. 'I still do,' Lorenzo said. 'But I've learned a lot from Indi. Sometimes, to really connect with people and make a difference, you have to be a bit more flexible.'

'She taught you that?' His grandfather looked thoughtful. 'She sounds an intriguing young woman.'

'She is.' Lorenzo smiled. 'I'll call her and arrange it.'

There was a gentle but insistent rap on the door. 'Indi? Indi, are you all right? Can I come in?'

Lottie.

Should she lie and pretend that she had a crashing headache?

But Lottie was perceptive. Even if Indigo could stall her for now, Lottie would notice that something was up. And she was a close enough and old enough friend to ask what was wrong.

'Come in,' she croaked.

'Indi, you've been crying,' Lottie said as she walked in and closed the door behind her.

Indigo felt the tears well up and forced them back.

'Sweetie, what's wrong?' Lottie asked. 'Is this to do with Lorenzo?'

'Sort of,' she hedged.

Lottie hugged her. 'I know you're missing him. Look, do you want Gus to have a word with him?'

'No, I'll be fine.' Indigo shook her head. 'I'll pull myself together.'

'Why don't you go to Melvante and see him?'

She blew out a breath. 'I can't do that. He's busy preparing to be king.'

'But you're missing him, and I bet he's missing you just as much.'

'We agreed it was just a fling and we were both going to walk away at the end.'

Lottie raised her eyebrows. 'I think it was more than just a fling. You fell for him, didn't you?'

Indigo bit her lip. 'Is it that obvious?'

'Sweetie, you two might have thought you were being discreet, but it was obvious to everyone,' Lottie said, squeezing her hand. 'You both always seemed to disappear at the same time, so we knew you were together—and the way you looked at each other across a room was, well…' She fanned herself. 'Scorching.'

'Oh.' Indigo felt the colour flood into her face. 'Sorry. We didn't mean to—' Then, to her horror, she burst into tears.

Lottie held her close and let her cry.

'Sorry. I'm being really wet,' she apologised.

'No, you've been alone for a long time and you just fell in love with Lorenzo.'

'He's the worst person I could fall in love with.'

'I can think of worse,' Lottie said darkly. 'Besides, Lorenzo's one of the good guys. Actually, Gus has already had the big-brother talk with him about you.'

Indigo scrubbed away the tears. 'That's so sweet of him.'

'Gus thinks of you as his other little sister. Actually, you're the sister I would've chosen, if I'd been able to.'

Indigo sniffed. 'Don't, Lottie, you'll make me cry even more.'

'What is it, Indi?'

She dragged in a breath. 'I don't know where to start.'

'Try the beginning—or the middle, if it's easier. Or just cut to the difficult bit and come straight out with it,' Lottie suggested.

'The difficult bit.' Indigo raked a hand through her hair. Well, she'd been here before. And Lottie had listened before. She was a safe person to tell. 'I'm pregnant.'

Lottie placed a hand on her shoulder. 'Indi, are you sure? You're not just late because you're stressed about Lorenzo going back to Melvante?'

'I'm sure.' Her breath hitched. 'I did a test. Three days ago.'

'You've known about this for *three days* and you didn't tell me?' Lottie looked hurt.

'I didn't want to dump it on you like I did last time, and I'm—I'm—oh, God, I'm so sorry.' She felt her face crumple again.

'Stop apologising. You're not dumping it on me. That's what friends are for, and I know you'd be there for me if it was the other way round.' Lottie hugged her again. 'So what do you want to do?'

'I don't know what to do for the best.' Three sleepless nights hadn't helped her decide a single thing. 'I mean, I have to tell Lorenzo—of course I do, it wouldn't be fair to keep the news to myself—but I'm not expecting anything from him.'

'He's not Nigel the Scumbag. He's an honourable man.'

'That's the point, Lottie. He's about to become the King of Melvante. Having an illegitimate child just isn't going to work for him.'

Lottie spread her hands. 'So make the child legitimate and marry the man. You and Lorenzo are crazy about each other.'

'But I won't fit into his world.' Indigo sighed. 'And it'll be like living in a goldfish bowl, with everyone watching what I do all the time. I can't just decide to go to the park or the beach because it's a glorious day. His schedules are mapped out months in advance and there are security people everywhere. I don't want that kind of life for me or for my baby.'

'What about what Lorenzo wants?' Lottie asked.

'He's got enough on his plate without having to deal with a baby.'

'Indi…you're not thinking…?' Lottie looked horrified.

Indigo shook her head. 'I haven't exactly slept well for the last three nights. I've had time to think about it. And I'm going to make the same decision as I made last time.' She dragged in a breath. '*Last time.* And we both know what happened then. Who's to say this won't resolve itself in the same way?'

'You lost the baby then, but it doesn't mean to say you're going to lose this baby. Right now, what you need,' Lottie said, 'is to see a doctor and get checked over. Get all the blood tests done and what have you. And I'll come with you to hold your hand.'

'I can't ask you to do that.'

'You're not asking—I'm telling you,' Lottie said. 'And, for once, that independent streak of yours is going to have to shut up and listen. Right?'

Indigo gave her a watery smile. 'Right.'

When Indigo came out of the doctor's surgery—with her pregnancy confirmed and a dating scan booked in at the hospital—she switched on her phone.

The message flashed up onto the screen: two missed calls. Both from Lorenzo. And there was a voicemail from him asking if she could give him a call.

She swallowed hard. How stupid to find herself almost in tears just at hearing his voice. That had to be the hormones whizzing round her system. She really wasn't that pathetic and needy.

Why did he want her to call him? Surely he didn't…?

She shook herself. No. Of *course* he didn't have any idea about the situation she was in right now. He couldn't read her mind, and she knew that Lottie wouldn't have betrayed her confidence.

Returning his call would at least give her the chance to talk to him. Maybe she'd get an opening to broach the subject of the baby. Not that telling him on the phone was ideal, but talking to him would be a start. She could see how he sounded and play it by ear.

Once back in the privacy of her car, she rang Lorenzo. Although she'd half expected to end up leaving a message on his voicemail, he answered immediately. 'Indi. Hello. Thanks for calling back.'

'You're welcome.' And she was *not* going to burst into tears. She played it as cool as she could. 'What can I do for you?'

'I have a commission for you. In Melvante. I was thinking maybe a rose window.'

Her dream job. She'd talked to him about what she'd love to create, given the chance. And he was offering her that chance—albeit in his home, rather than her own.

'Would this be in the palace?' she asked tentatively.

'Yes. It's for the coronation. I know it's ridiculously short notice, but do you think you could fit it in?'

So he wanted her to work for him?

How naive she'd been, thinking that he might've wanted just to talk to her. After all, he'd asked her to make their fling permanent and she'd turned him down. He had no reason to think she might have changed her mind or regretted the decision. Their affair was over and life had moved on; he was about to become king. And he even sounded different—slightly more formal and a little distant. Which made what she needed to tell him even more difficult. Just how was she going to bring up something so emotional, when all he wanted to talk to her about was work?

'I could look at where you want to site it and come up with some designs, yes,' she said carefully. She had some more projects scheduled in for when she'd finished at Edensfield, but she was pretty sure that her clients would be flexible about the timescales if she asked them nicely. 'When were you thinking?'

'Tomorrow?' he suggested.

'Sorry, I really can't. I'm fitting the mermaid window back into place at Edensfield tomorrow.'

'How about the day after?'

'The day after is fine,' she said. Though he'd forgotten one crucial little detail. 'Provided I can book a flight. If there isn't one available, it might have to be later.'

'You don't need to book a flight.'

'As a mere mortal,' she said crisply, 'I don't actually have wings to get me to Melvante under my own steam.'

'I didn't mean that. I meant, I'll get it arranged for you.' He laughed. 'Oh, Indi. I've missed your straight talking.'

Maybe. But he clearly didn't miss *her*.

As if he could read her thoughts, he said softly, 'But not as much as I've missed you.'

She had to swallow really, really hard. Because right then she really, really missed him. Talking to him and knowing that he was hundreds of miles away was sheer torture.

'Come to Melvante,' he said, his voice as warm and tempting as melted chocolate.

'Because you want me to design some glass for you?'

She regretted the words as soon as they were out, knowing how needy they made her sound. And she didn't want Lorenzo to think she was pathetic.

'The commission's genuine,' he said, 'and I'll pay the going rate—I'm not expecting you to give me some ridiculously huge discount. But I guess it's also an excuse to see you.'

And she really needed to see him. Oh, God. The idea of Lorenzo wrapping his arms round her and holding her close, telling her not to worry and that everything would be OK because he loved her...

But how could he possibly do that? He was about to become the King of Melvante. She knew Lorenzo was attracted to her, and she knew he liked her. Maybe the two together made up love. Though Indigo had learned not to trust love, because in her experience it just ended in heartache. Nigel had dumped her as soon as he'd discovered that she was pregnant, and then she'd found out how deep his betrayal had been. OK, so Lorenzo wasn't a cheat and a liar—but, even so, how could he possibly support her and the baby, with all that he had going on in his life right now? Plus the press would have a field day if they found out that the new King of Melvante was going to have a love-child with a woman who was the illegitimate daughter of an earl...

She couldn't see any way out of it. Lorenzo had to follow his duty, and that would mean dumping her because she was totally unsuitable to be a queen. And, even if her life hadn't been so tarnished in the past, there was the fact that he'd live the rest of his life in the glare of the public eye—which wasn't what she wanted for herself or for the baby.

'Indi? Are you still there?' he asked.

'It's a bad connection,' she lied.

'OK. I'll get Salvatore to call you with the flight details and an agenda.'

'Who's Salvatore?'

'My assistant. I'll see you the day after tomorrow. *Ciao.*'

He hung up, and Indi stared at her phone. This didn't seem real. She'd just agreed to go to Melvante and see him. And the way he'd dropped so easily into speaking Italian at the end of their conversation… Well, it wasn't surprising. He was right where he belonged, in his European kingdom. While she belonged here in England. And she had a nasty feeling that the distance between them now wasn't just geographical.

CHAPTER TEN

LATER THAT AFTERNOON, Indigo's phone rang. She didn't recognise the number on the screen and almost didn't answer it, assuming it was some cold-caller; then again, Lorenzo had said that his assistant would contact her about the flights. Maybe it was him.

She answered the phone warily. 'Hello?'

'Signorina Moran?' The stranger's voice had a very slight accent, something which sounded as if it came from the southern Mediterranean.

'Yes,' she said. 'Who's calling?'

'My name is Salvatore Pozzi. I'm the personal assistant to His Royal Highness Prince Lorenzo of Melvante. He asked me to get in touch with you with the details of your flight.'

'Thank you.' Oh, and how formal was this guy? No wonder Lorenzo was so buttoned up if this was the way things were in Melvante. The chances were that she wouldn't fit into his private world, either, she thought with a sinking heart.

'Do you have an email address so I can send you the information and the agenda for meeting His Royal Highness?' Salvatore asked.

Agenda? Meeting?

It all felt very cool, very brisk—and it was the total opposite to what she'd shared with Lorenzo here in England.

Well, it was her own fault for blurring the lines between business and personal stuff. Here at Edensfield, they'd been in a bubble, protected from the rest of the world. In Melvante, Lorenzo was in the full glare of the public eye. A business meeting with him was the best she could hope for. And what he'd said about missing her—maybe he did, but things were different now and she knew he couldn't afford to act on those feelings.

'Yes, I have an email address.' She dictated it coolly and professionally. Because, after all, this was a job. She was planning to meet her client, not her lover. And she'd better keep that in mind if she wanted to keep what was left of her heart intact.

'*Bene*. Good. I'll email you now. If there are any problems or you have any questions when you've read through the details, please call me.'

'I will. And thank you for your help,' she said.

'My pleasure, Signorina Moran.' Though there wasn't really any warmth in his voice. It was just politeness.

By the time she'd powered up her laptop, the email from Salvatore was waiting in her in-box. Her flight was at ten a.m. the day after tomorrow—from the local airport rather than one of the larger London airports, so she guessed there would probably be a connecting flight somewhere in Europe. And there was an agenda giving her times when the prince would be meeting her over the next few days. A briefing meeting. A tour of the castle. A tour of the cathedral. A status update. A meeting with His Majesty King Lorenzo II and His Royal Highness Prince Lorenzo to discuss final details—*oh, help*. Not just Lorenzo, then. His grandfather as well. And his grandfather definitely wouldn't approve of her.

Everything was tightly scheduled, she noticed, down to the minute. Well, obviously Lorenzo had a thousand and one demands on his time right now. She was lucky he was giving her this much time.

But just when was she going to get the chance to tell him about the baby?

She blew out a breath. She'd definitely have to play that one by ear. But at least she had enough time in between those meetings to work on the designs and come up with something she hoped would do him justice.

She finished scanning the list. Charity ball? What? Why on earth did he want her to go to that? Oh, for pity's sake. He must know she wasn't the kind of person who went to glamorous events like charity balls. She was a glass geek who was more likely to go to an exhibition or find the nearest art gallery or medieval church.

Apart from the fact that Lorenzo had made it very clear he was busy—otherwise he would've called her himself with the flight details and he wouldn't have asked his assistant to send her an agenda—Indigo didn't trust her voice not to wobble when she spoke to him. Salvatore had said to call him with any queries, but this one was a little bit too personal. So she sent Salvatore a brief, polite email thanking him for the information, then texted Lorenzo. Why is there a charity ball on the agenda?

t took him a while to respond. Probably, she thought, because he was in a meeting and there would be tons of other messages on his phone. Assuming he didn't just forward everything to his assistant to deal with; and then the fact that she'd texted the prince instead of contacting his assistant wouldn't go down too well.

Too late, now. She couldn't recall the message.

She was just finishing up a last piece of work on the mermaid window when her phone beeped to signal a text. She made herself wait to read it and not rush straight to it. So you can meet some of the people of my country, get more of a feel for the background. Are you worried about it?

Trust him to pick up on that. Of course not. she lied.

Of course she was worried about attending a charity ball in Melvante. Even though she'd be there as a business associate, there was still a chance that people might guess that her relationship with Lorenzo hadn't been strictly business in England.

Just checking the dress code, she typed.even though she was pretty sure she knew what it was already.

Black tie, he responded.

Which meant a ball gown. Something she didn't own. Luckily, she knew two people who did and who'd be prepared to lend her one—and they were both here in this house, which would save her a rushed journey. OK. Thanks.

He didn't text her back, this time. Super-busy, she guessed. Still. At least she was going to see him. And she would have plenty of time in Melvante to think, to work out how to tell him about the baby.

Funny how just talking to Indigo had made him antsy, Lorenzo thought. It brought home to him how much he'd missed her. How much he wanted to see her.

But she'd sounded very cool, calm and businesslike on the phone. So was she going to treat this as just another commission, or was she using it as an excuse to see him— the way he was using it as an excuse to see her?

He really couldn't tell.

So he'd just have to compartmentalise things and

keep his feelings separate. Maybe he'd be able to tell more when he saw her.

Work kept Indigo occupied for the rest of the day; she spent the evening looking up everything she could about Melvante and making notes. The next day was spent putting the mermaid window in place; and then it was time to pack. Just as well, she thought, that she had her passport with her; she and Lottie had spent a girly weekend in Paris just before she'd started work on the window, and she'd gone to Edensfield from Paris rather than via her flat in London.

'I'll drive you to the airport—I've got stuff to do in town anyway, so it's not very far out of my way. And you can leave all your stuff here while you're in Melvante. You need to be back here for the official unveiling of the window, in any case,' Lottie told her.

'Thanks.' She paused. 'Lottie, I meant to ask you last night—can I borrow a ball gown, please?'

'A ball gown?' Lottie looked surprised.

'Lorenzo wants me to attend a charity ball. He says it's good background for designing his window.'

Lottie raised an eyebrow. 'He must live on a different planet.'

One where Indigo knew she wouldn't fit in. 'I guess.'

'Of course you can borrow a ball gown. Come and raid my wardrobe.'

Doing something girly helped to occupy Indigo's mind for a little while, but once she'd chosen a plain black ball gown—one she intended to wear with her red strappy shoes, to give her a bit of courage—and packed some business suits, her mind went back to Lorenzo. How was he going to react to her? And how would he react to the news about the baby?

Worry kept her awake for most of the night, having endless conversations in her head with him. And she couldn't even drink coffee to keep her awake, the next morning—apart from the fact that it wouldn't be good for the baby, the smell of it made her feel queasy. Maybe she could have a nap on the plane or something.

She didn't say much on the way to the airport; her stomach felt as if it was tied in knots and panic rather than blood was flowing through her veins. But she made an effort when Lottie dropped her off.

'Thanks, Lottie.' Indigo hugged her. 'I'll text you when I get there.'

'Good. And remember, Indi, Lorenzo's not Nigel. He's not going to abandon you.'

'I know.' Though he might not actually have a choice in the matter, Indigo thought. He might *have* to abandon her.

Why couldn't she have fallen for a man who didn't come with complications?

At the customer services desk, she said to the assistant, 'I think I have a ticket to pick up?' She gave her name and the flight number.

'Of course, Madam. This way.'

To Indigo's surprise, she was waved straight through Customs. There were none of the usual checks she was used to—not even her passport, much less having her bag X-rayed and walking through a scanner. What was going on?

When she was escorted out to the runway, she saw a small private jet.

What?

'Is there—well—some mistake?' she asked. 'I was expecting a connecting flight to Melvante.'

'There's no connection needed, Madam,' the attendant told her. 'This is the Melvante royal plane.'

Lorenzo had sent the royal plane for her? But...

'I—um—thank you,' she said, flustered. No wonder he'd said that she wouldn't need to sort out a flight. This one was just for her. Which was crazy. She barely even travelled first class, let alone in super-luxury. This wasn't the kind of life she was used to.

Clutching her suitcase, she walked up the steps to the door of the plane, where a woman in a smart navy suit greeted her.

'Good morning, *signorina*. My name is Maria, and I'm your flight attendant today. Let me take your luggage.'

Indigo had to blink twice as she stepped into the aisle. This was nothing like the kind of planes she'd flown in before, with slightly cramped seats and a narrow aisle. This was more like a hotel business suite than a plane. There were cream leather sofas at one end, and a table at the other end which looked as if it belonged in a board room together with the deeply padded chairs. There was even an arrangement of fresh flowers on a coffee table.

'His Royal Highness asked us to make sure you were comfortable on your journey, *signorina*,' Maria said, ushering her over to one of the sofas. 'May I get you something to eat or drink?'

'A glass of water would be lovely, please, Maria,' Indigo said, summoning a smile. Right at that moment she felt very much out of her depth. Lorenzo hadn't sent her a plane ticket—he'd sent her a *plane*. How unreal was that?

'Can I offer you a magazine?'

Indigo shook her head. 'That's very kind of you, but I was actually planning to do some work.'

'Of course. You're very welcome to use the table, if you prefer it to the sofas. There are plugs if you need them to charge a laptop.'

'Thank you, Maria,' she said, and settled herself at the table.

When Maria returned with a glass of water, Indigo noticed that it had ice and a slice of lime too. And the glass was lead crystal rather than the disposable plastic cups she was used to seeing on a plane.

'If you wish for anything, please ring the bell and I'll come straight away,' Maria said.

'Thank you, Maria.' Indigo tried out some of the Italian she'd learned over the last day or so. *'Mille grazie.'*

Maria's smile showed her how much the gesture was appreciated.

So this was what a royal lifestyle meant. The ultimate in comfort and convenience. And yet it wasn't super-flashy; the room had a businesslike air.

And she'd better remember that she was going to be in Melvante on business, first and foremost.

She read through the file she'd made on Melvante, the day before, and made some more notes for possible designs. The flight went incredibly quickly; at the airport in Melvante, she was also waved straight through Customs with no passport check. Then again, she supposed, if you were travelling on the king's private plane, that kind of guaranteed you were expected and welcome in the country.

There was a car waiting for her; she recognised the chauffeur standing outside. 'Bruno! How lovely to see you.'

'And you, too, Signorina Moran,' he said with a formal little bow.

'It's Indi to you, as you know very well,' she said with a smile, and gave him a hug that made him blush.

When Bruno opened the rear door for her, she asked, 'Can I be cheeky and ask if I can sit in the front with you, please, Bruno? All this…' She grimaced. 'It's a little bit overwhelming.'

'Of course, *signo*—' he began, then with a smile corrected himself. 'Indi.' He opened the door for her and waited for her to settle before closing it again and going round to the driver's side.

Indigo had seen a similar large black diplomatic car with tinted windows at Edensfield, but Bruno hadn't been in livery there. Here, he wore a smart uniform with gold braid and a cap, and he looked every inch a royal chauffeur. This was feeling more and more unreal with every second.

In a different life, Lorenzo might have met her at the airport himself. He might have run towards her, lifted her off her feet, swung her round, and kissed her until they were both dizzy.

But Lorenzo in England wasn't the same as Lorenzo in Melvante. Here, he was about to become the king. And it most definitely wasn't suitable for a king to meet a contractor at the airport, much less greet her with such warmth.

How would he greet her when the schedule said he'd meet her? Would he be cool, calm, collected and distant? Or would he still be the man he'd been in England, passionate once his defences were down?

She damped down the panic. 'I assume His Royal Highness is in a meeting?'

'He's always in meetings,' Bruno said. 'He works harder than anyone I know.'

That didn't surprise her. She knew that Lorenzo had a strong sense of duty, and she respected that. 'Uh-huh,' she said.

Although Indigo could normally chat to anyone, and she'd chatted quite happily to Bruno at Edensfield, right now she was feeling ever so slightly intimidated. As they drove through the city towards the castle, she could see that it was just as Lorenzo had said: a picture-postcard style white stone castle with turrets and pointy tiled roofs. Had she been visiting the place on holiday, she would have thought it pretty. But, at that moment, it felt as if it towered over her disapprovingly.

Bruno parked the car on the gravel outside the castle, opened the door for her and took her bag, then ushered her in to the castle through what she guessed was the equivalent of the tradesman's entrance.

He took her through to an office; as she stepped onto the carpet, her feet sank into it. Everywhere was polished wood and gilt—like the office of a CEO in a major company. Which, Indigo supposed, was effectively Lorenzo's position. Only his 'company' happened to be a country.

A middle-aged man in a three-piece suit looked up from behind his mahogany desk as the door opened, and stood up. He said something swiftly in Italian to Bruno—too fast for Indigo to translate, with her meagre stock of tourist vocabulary—and inclined his head at her. 'Good afternoon, Signorina Moran. I am Salvatore Pozzi.'

'Good afternoon, Signor Pozzi.' She stepped forward and offered her hand; and when he took it she made sure that her handshake was firm and businesslike. 'Thank you for arranging my flight and the car here.'

'No problem.' Though he still wasn't smiling.

'Bye, Bruno,' she said as the chauffeur left, sketching her a salute. It felt as if her only friend in the place had gone. Salvatore was perfectly polite, but his expression was inscrutable. Indigo had no idea what Lorenzo had told him about her, or if he knew about their fling back in England.

The only thing she could think to talk about was business. 'The agenda says that I am to meet—' Hmm, so how did she refer to the prince in front of his assistant? She could hardly call him by his first name—not in such formal surroundings. 'His Royal Highness,' she finished, 'at three.'

'I am afraid His Royal Highness's meeting is running a little late. But if you would care to wait in the sitting room, *signorina*, I can arrange for some tea to be brought to you.'

'Thank you, but I'm fine. Please don't feel you have to order tea.'

'As you wish, *signorina*.' Salvatore led her through to another room. There was still the same deep carpet, exquisite furnishings and silk drapes at the window. It really brought it home to Indigo that she was in a palace, not just a normal office or home.

'Please sit down.' Salvatore indicated the sofa.

Just then a dog burst through the doorway, trotted over to them with his tail a wagging blur, and sniffed at her.

'Caesar!' Salvatore scolded. 'Bad dog—you shouldn't be in here.'

'Lorenzo's favourite spaniel. The one who sneaks onto sofas.' Indigo smiled, remembering what he'd told her about the palace dogs.

Salvatore looked surprised, and she realised what she'd just said. 'I mean, um, His Royal Highness's spaniel,' she corrected herself swiftly.

He looked slightly less disapproving now she'd remembered her place and resumed formal protocol. 'Yes.'

'I like dogs,' she offered. And at least having a dog to make a fuss of would give her something else to think about instead of worrying how it would be when Lorenzo finally came out of his meeting to see her again. 'I don't mind if he stays.'

Again, that cool inscrutable expression. 'If you're sure, *signorina.*'

'I'm sure.' She sat down. 'Come and sit with me, Caesar.'

The dog gave a happy wriggle at the sound of his name and trotted over to the sofa.

Salvatore gave a brief nod. 'I will call you as soon as His Royal Highness Prince Lorenzo is ready to see you.'

'Mille grazie,' she said, but Salvatore didn't seem as impressed as Maria had been by her effort to speak Italian. He just gave another of those curt little nods and left.

'So it's just you and me, Caesar,' she said.

The dog wagged his tail and put his paws on her knee.

'I'm really glad you're here,' she said. 'Because I have no idea how your master's going to react to me. Whether he meant it about missing me, or whether he just wants me to design a window for him—I haven't a clue.' Lottie had said that Lorenzo wasn't like Nigel, and Indigo knew that was true; at least his first words when she told him about the baby wouldn't be to demand that she had a termination.

But as to how he'd really feel, what he'd say…

She swallowed hard. 'And how he's going to react to my news—that scares me even more. I don't fit in here. I might be the daughter of an earl, but I didn't grow up in his world and I'm no Cinderella. I'd be much happier in the kitchen, chatting to the cooks and swapping recipes for cake.'

Caesar licked her hand.

'I guess it's a matter of wait and see,' she said, and leaned back against the back of the sofa.

Twenty minutes later, Lorenzo walked into the sitting room to discover Indigo fast asleep on the sofa, with Caesar curled up on the sofa in the space behind her knees. She looked exhausted, with dark hollows under her eyes.

Clearly she'd been pushing herself as hard as he'd been pushing himself.

Part of him really wanted to wake her with a kiss, to see those gorgeous blue eyes open and see her smile at him. But part of him thought it would be kinder just to let her rest. He found a blanket and tucked it round her.

'Keep an eye on her, Caesar,' he said softly, and the dog wagged his tail ever so gently, as if trying not to wake her.

'Your Royal Highness, would you like me to—?' Salvatore began.

'No, let her sleep for a bit longer,' Lorenzo said quietly. 'I'll work on my laptop in here for a while.'

CHAPTER ELEVEN

INDIGO WOKE WITH a start, and realised that there was a blanket tucked round her and Lorenzo's spaniel was curled into the crook of her knees. The dog stretched and yawned as she struggled to a sitting position, trying to get her head straight. There definitely hadn't been a blanket anywhere near her. Who had tucked her in like that? She didn't think it would've been Salvatore, who had been cool with her to the point of disapproval. And she was probably late for her meeting with Lorenzo now.

Oh, great. Her first day at the palace, and it had been a total disaster so far.

She glanced at her watch. Not just late—she'd missed the entire meeting.

'Oh, you *idiot*,' she groaned.

'Why am I an idiot?'

She looked over to where the voice had come from.

Lorenzo was sitting in the chair opposite, working on his laptop.

For a second, the world spun. Was this the man who'd been so passionate in England, or was this the king-to-be? She erred on the side of caution. 'Your Royal Highness. I'm so sorry.'

He smiled. 'Don't be. You clearly needed that nap. Been working stupid hours, have we?'

'Pots and kettles. You have bags under your—' She stopped abruptly. This wasn't Edensfield, where they'd both been friends of the family and on an equal footing—where he'd been her lover and she could tease him with impunity. This was Melvante, where he was her client and he was also about to become the head of the country. Which meant she had to deal with him in a completely different way. 'Sorry, Your Royal Highness,' she muttered.

'You really are different, out of England.' His eyes crinkled at the corners. 'Do you think I'm going to have you thrown into the palace dungeons for insubordination, or something?'

'Are there palace dungeons?'

He laughed. 'Yes, but they're not used. We have a progressive judicial system. Lighten up, Indi. I was teasing you.' He smiled. 'Besides, it was cute when you snored in tandem with Caesar.'

He was still teasing her. Which ought to be a good sign. But Indigo was still feeling groggy from her nap, and the secret she had to tell him felt as if it was gripping her in a vice. She had to tell him the truth—but not until she'd worked out the right words to use and the right time to say them.

'I'm sorry,' she said again. 'It was totally unprofessional of me to fall asleep like that.'

'You'd been travelling, and I'd guess you've been working nonstop over the last few days.'

'I have,' she admitted. And she'd missed him, so much. Part of her really wanted to walk over to him, wrap her arms round him, kiss him and tell him how glad she was to see him. Yet, despite the fact that they were in the same room, there was still a huge gulf between them. She couldn't even call him by his given name, because she was too aware of who he was: the future King of Melvante.

What a mess.

'Have I made you late for your next appointment?' she asked.

'No. Salvatore has rearranged my diary slightly.'

Which made her feel even more guilty. And it was another reason for Lorenzo's assistant to disapprove of her. 'Why didn't you just wake me up?'

'Because you looked comfortable.'

'Did you tuck me in?'

He nodded. 'And Caesar was happy to keep you company.'

'He's a nice dog.'

'He's horribly spoiled,' Lorenzo said, but his tone was indulgent.

If only he'd just come over to her and hold her close. How could they be in the same room and yet the gap between them feel wider than the geographical distance when they'd been in different countries?

'I, um, forgot to ask Salvatore which hotel he'd booked me into,' she said. And she really hoped it was one with a reasonable tariff, rather than a super-luxury one with an astronomical room rate. Her finances wouldn't run to the kind of places that Lorenzo would stay.

'You're not. You're staying at the palace.'

Staying with him?

For one mad moment, she thought he was telling her that this was going to be just like Edensfield, and they'd spend their nights curled up together and wake in each other's arms. Then common sense kicked in as he began speaking.

'We have several apartments for guests.'

'I'm not really a guest,' she said. 'I'm here to work.'

'Maybe a bit of both,' he said. 'Come on, I'll take you to your suite.'

And maybe there, in private, he'd be different with her.

She damped down the flicker of hope before she got too carried away. Of course he wouldn't. He was about to be the king. He didn't have time for this.

'Where's your suitcase?'

A prince most definitely couldn't wait on her. 'It's light. I'll carry it myself.' And she gave him a look just to make quite sure he knew she meant it; she was used to relying on herself, and that was the way it would continue to be.

'As you wish,' he said coolly, and she wished she hadn't been quite so quick to knock back his offer. He came from such a formal, restricted world. How would he know how to be anything else?

She still felt faintly groggy, but she followed him through the corridors with the little dog trotting along beside them. Lorenzo stopped by a door and opened it. 'Your suite. I'll let you freshen up.'

So he wasn't planning to spend too much time in private with her, then. She was really in danger of misreading everything. Best to keep it cool, calm and super-professional. 'Thank you very much. Perhaps we can reschedule our briefing meeting.'

'Of course. You still have my mobile phone number, yes?' At her nod, he said, 'Call me when you're ready and I'll come and collect you. Not because you're a prisoner, but because the castle's a bit of a maze and until you know your way around it can be a bit daunting.'

'Thank you.' Not that she was ever going to get to know her way around this castle.

He kissed her lightly on the cheek. 'Come on, Caesar. We need to let Indi settle in,' he told the spaniel, who gave Indigo a mournful look, but followed him down the corridor.

When he'd left, Indigo explored the suite. The sitting room was huge, with a sofa, coffee table and a couple of armchairs. There was a shelf of books in a variety of languages, a television and a state of the art music system. The bathroom was just acres of marble, with the most enormous walk-in shower, a deep bath and thick fluffy towels. The bedroom held a huge oak four-poster bed, with a wardrobe running the length of the room, a cheval mirror and a chest of drawers. She opened the wardrobe doors and hung up her clothes neatly. A couple of business suits, a couple of pairs of jeans, and Lottie's ball gown; and how meagre her outfits looked in that enormous space. Even if she'd had her entire wardrobe with her, her clothes wouldn't have made much impression.

The pillows looked deep and soft and inviting; she glanced longingly at them, then shook herself. She'd already made enough of a fool of herself, falling asleep on Lorenzo's sofa while she was waiting for his meeting to finish. If she let herself give in to the demands of her pregnancy now and slept again… Well. Lorenzo was sharp. He noticed little details. And she wasn't ready for him to put them all together and work it out for himself. She wanted to tell him the news herself.

Just not quite yet.

She showered and freshened up, then called Lorenzo's mobile.

It went straight to voicemail. Which wasn't so surprising.

'It's Indi. The time's four-thirty in the afternoon. I'm ready whenever you are,' she said, then hung up. She had no idea how long he'd be. But, given that she'd slept straight through their meeting, she was hardly in a position to demand anything.

She worked on her laptop for a while, until there was a knock at the door.

'Come in,' she called.

Lorenzo walked in, with Caesar at his heels. 'Sorry to keep you waiting.'

'No problem. I know you're busy.'

He inclined his head in acknowledgement. 'I meant to ask you, is there anything you'd like for dinner tonight so I can tell chef?'

'Anything, really,' she said, not wanting to be difficult. As long as it didn't have a strong smell. Not that she could explain to him why she wanted bland food without opening up a conversation at totally the wrong time. 'I wasn't expecting you to feed me.'

He smiled at her. 'We're not going to starve you, Indi. I wish I had time to have dinner with you tonight myself, but something's cropped up.'

'It's fine,' she said. Of course he wouldn't have dinner with any of his contractors. Not unless it was scheduled in and rubber-stamped by Salvatore.

'I would have asked you to come with me this evening, but it's state business and it'll be horribly dull.'

At least she would still have been with him, but never mind. She damped down the hurt. 'I know you're up to your eyes,' she said softly. 'It's OK.'

Just for a second, the formality in his face vanished and he looked lonely and lost, as if she was the first person who'd actually noticed that he was struggling to deal with everything. And, after all, it was a huge weight he was about to shoulder, becoming the state leader of his country.

Then the moment passed and Lorenzo was back to being His Royal Highness, ever so slightly remote and aloof. 'Is there anything else you need?'

Only for you to hold me and tell me that everything's going to be all right, she thought. But she knew she couldn't ask for that. Better to stick to business. 'It'd be useful to see the room where the window will be sited.'

'Of course. I can take you there now.'

'That would be good. I'll bring my equipment so I can measure up and take photographs.' Then she grimaced, remembering how he'd been about photographs at Edensfield. 'That is allowed, yes?'

'I'm not going to make you hand over your camera or delete the files,' he said with a smile, clearly remembering their first meeting too.

'And they won't go anywhere but my computer—I won't download them anywhere,' she said.

'I know. But thank you for the reassurance.'

Once she'd gathered her camera, notepad and laptop together, Lorenzo ushered her down the corridor.

Everywhere there were thick carpets and wood panelling; and all the surfaces were so shiny that it was clear there must be a huge number of staff all dusting and polishing the castle to perfection.

'State dining room,' he said, opening one door and letting her peek inside.

Solid gold cutlery, was Indigo's first thought. Followed by *solid gold candelabra.*

She was used to opulence, from her visits to Edensfield, but this was another world entirely. And she'd just bet the crystal glasses were antique, just as any meal served at that table would be presented on antique porcelain.

'Drawing room,' he said, showing her the next room. She glanced at the comfortable upholstered chairs, antique occasional tables and arrangements of fresh flowers—and then stopped dead. 'Is that a Burne-Jones over there on the wall?'

He nodded. 'It's the portrait of my great-great-grandmother I told you about.'

'May I?'

'Of course.'

She walked over to it and studied it for a while. 'It's beautiful—you're very lucky.'

'Salvatore knows a lot about our art collection. Talk to him tomorrow. He'll show you round when he has a moment.'

She didn't think that Salvatore would unbend enough with her to do that, but smiled politely. 'Thank you.'

Finally Lorenzo led her to a room at the very end of a corridor. 'This is where we thought the window could be sited—in the library.'

Like the mermaid window at Edensfield, she thought, and was filled with wistfulness. She would love to have the Lorenzo from Edensfield back rather than the formal, very polite and very guarded stranger walking next to her.

'This is one of my favourite rooms in the house,' he said as he ushered her into a long room.

The two longest walls were lined with books in dark wooden cases with glass fronts and a sliding wooden ladder, so anyone who wanted a book from the upper shelves could reach them. But there were also a couple of leather chesterfields and a low coffee table with a chessboard on it. There was a desk sited in front of a large window with a number of gold-framed photographs—and she'd bet it was solid gold, not gilt framing—and a grand piano in the centre of the room.

And that, she thought, was why it was Lorenzo's favourite room. No doubt he spent as much time at that piano as he could. Which wouldn't be very much, now.

The spaniel pattered over to the fireplace and stretched out on the rug, clearly used to being there.

There were some stained-glass windows at the far end of the room. 'Is that where you want the new window?' she asked.

'Yes.'

As they passed the desk, she glanced out of the window and saw the rose garden. 'Oh, that's gorgeous,' she said, noting the way the colours of the roses blended. 'It's like a rainbow of roses.'

He looked out. 'I've never really noticed that before, but you're right.' He smiled at her. 'Funny, I thought I knew everything about the castle, but you're making me see it with new eyes.'

There wasn't much she could say to that. She distracted herself by taking a couple of photographs and making a couple of sketches. And, unsurprisingly, he had half a dozen messages on his phone that he needed to answer.

He'd just finished with them when she took out her tape measure. 'Need a hand measuring?' he asked.

'If you don't mind,' she said. 'That would be helpful.'

But, as she finished the last section, his hand touched hers briefly, and it felt like electricity coursing through her veins.

'Indi,' he whispered.

She looked up at him and he dipped his head, brushing his mouth against hers. She closed her eyes as he deepened the kiss.

God, she'd missed this so much. Missed *him* so much that she felt the tears stinging her eyelids.

And then she dropped the tape measure.

On his foot.

He broke the kiss and retrieved her tape measure. 'I'm sorry,' he said. 'I probably shouldn't have done that.'

She knew what he meant. The attraction was still there. The same feelings they'd had for each other back at Edensfield. But this was a different world and he just wasn't free to give in to those feelings.

Which made it even harder for her to tell him about the baby; she knew he had such a strong sense of duty and he'd want to marry her for the baby's sake. But she most definitely wasn't a suitable royal bride, so marriage was out of the question.

Time to back off—and to change the subject, before she said something stupid.

Be professional, she reminded herself. This is about your job.

'Would you mind sitting for a couple of portraits?' she asked. 'Photographs, I mean. I'm not going to make you sit for hours while I sketch you.'

He raised an eyebrow, as if remembering their conversation about the fairy tales with a twist. 'You really need to do that?'

'If I'm putting you in a stained-glass window, then the portrait needs to look like you,' she pointed out.

'I guess so.'

'And it would be useful to see your robes of state, or whatever it is that kings wear.' Not just because she could use them in a pose, but because it would remind her of who he was. That he was out of reach.

'Ceremonial robes,' he said.

'And a crown.' Just to hammer it home.

'We can do a crown,' he said, looking thoughtful.

'And where does all this happen? The cathedral?' She forced herself not to think about the fact that the cathedral would also be where he would eventually get married. To a suitable princess.

'Yes—and there's a special coronation chair. I'm scheduled to show you round tomorrow.' He met her gaze. 'Or Salvatore can, if you'd rather.'

It would probably be easier if Salvatore showed her round, she thought. Then she wouldn't slip up and say something inappropriate, because she'd remember who she was talking to and why she was here in Melvante. She'd have it at the front of her mind that this was strictly business and not because Lorenzo wanted her there.

But, to do her job fully, she needed to understand what was in his head. How did he feel about becoming king? And she'd slept through the briefing meeting, so she still had a dozen or more questions. She needed to know if they wanted him to look serene, statesmanlike, or what.

'I'd rather you showed me round, if you don't mind—that means we can catch up with the briefing meeting I missed, too. If you're sure you can spare the time,' she added quickly.

'I'll make sure I do.' His phone shrilled; he glanced at the screen and sighed. 'I'm sorry. I need to take this.'

'Don't worry, I'll find my own way back to my quarters.'

'Are you sure?'

She smiled, giving him her bravest face. 'If I get lost, I can always ask someone for directions.'

'OK. We'll talk later,' he said.

It was weird to be wandering through the palace on her own, Indigo thought as she left the library. She felt like a trespasser; she really didn't belong here. Lorenzo had said that the castle was home and he had happy memories of the place, but to her he looked tired and slightly strained. He'd retreated behind formality, apart from that brief kiss—and he'd apologised for that straight away, telling her outright that it had been a mistake.

Right at that moment, she couldn't see any common ground between them. It underlined how sensible she'd been to say no when he'd suggested continuing their affair. Lorenzo as a man—yes, she could trust him enough to fall in love with him. She already had. But His Royal Highness Lorenzo had so many walls up that it could never work.

She still had to tell him about the baby. It wouldn't be fair either to him or to the baby to keep that quiet. But no way was her baby growing up inside the walls of this quiet, formal, over-restrained palace. She wanted a home where a child could laugh and shout with joy—not an old-fashioned place where children were shut away in a nursery and should be seen and not heard.

CHAPTER TWELVE

THIS REALLY WASN'T going how Lorenzo had expected. Indigo was completely different, out here; she seemed nervous and quiet, not like the independent, sparky woman he'd fallen for in England.

He wanted to hold her and tell her how much he'd missed her. He wanted to kiss her again and feel her warmth seeping through him. But he also knew how his mother had felt so trapped at the palace, and he didn't want that for Indigo. No way would he push her into something that would make her unhappy.

And that was the final proof that he wasn't his father—because, if he had to, he was prepared to let Indi leave.

But first he was going to do his utmost to persuade her that sharing his life here wouldn't be so bad.

He raided the palace gardens before his meeting; afterwards, he grabbed a quick sandwich, then dropped in on Indigo. 'Sorry,' he said, handing her the flowers. 'I've been a rubbish host so far.'

She looked surprised. 'You didn't need to do that, but they're lovely. Thank you.' She breathed in their scent. 'And I understand that you're busy. The coronation's very soon and you have tons to do.'

'Yes, and Nonno's away for a few days—that's why I haven't introduced you to him yet.'

'I'm kind of nervous about meeting your grandfather,' she admitted.

'There's no need.' He spread his hands. 'Nonno's a pussycat.'

'He's a king,' she corrected.

'He's a man first,' Lorenzo said softly. Just as he was. But could Indigo learn to see that?

Indigo didn't want to fight with Lorenzo, so she said nothing, but she disagreed with him completely. If you were in that position, no matter how much you wanted to be seen as a person first, you'd always be seen as what you were rather than who you were. 'I'd better put these in water.'

He followed her into the kitchen and helped her find a couple of glasses to contain the flowers. 'Sorry. I didn't think this through properly. I should've brought you a vase as well.'

'No, I like that you were spontaneous. It's sweet,' she said.

'Just so you know, I wanted to meet you at the airport,' he said softly.

'It's fine. Bruno was there.' Though it warmed her that he *had* wanted to be with her. 'Besides, I'm here as a consultant, so people would think it strange if you met me at the airport.'

He shrugged. 'I guess.'

'Come and sit down—can I make you a drink or something?' She'd checked out the kitchenette and seen that there was a selection of tea and coffee, plus a supply of fresh milk in the small fridge.

He smiled. 'How come you manage to be a good hostess when you've only been here a few hours?'

She shrugged. 'It's just how I was brought up. You always offer someone a hot drink the second they walk through your door. Well, strictly speaking this is your door, not mine,' she amended, 'but you know what I mean.'

'Do you know what I want more than coffee, right now?' he asked.

'Mind-reading isn't one of my special skills,' she said.

'I know.' He laughed. 'OK. I'll tell you. I just want to hold you.'

'That isn't such a good idea,' she said. 'I'm here on business.'

'You're here because I wanted to see you, and right now I can't come to England, so bringing you here seemed like the best solution.'

'You sent a plane for me, Lorenzo. Don't you think that's a little bit flashy?' she asked.

'Probably,' he admitted, 'and it's bad for the environment as well. But, given that you're a mere mortal and don't possess wings…'

When he was like this, it would be so easy to give in and just be with him. He was adorable—sweet and funny, Lorenzo the man and not Lorenzo the Crown Prince.

'Hello, Indi,' he said softly, and kissed her.

She managed to stand her ground. Just. 'We can't do this, Lorenzo. We're not in England any more. You're about to become king.'

'And you're putting obstacles in the way. Why are you so scared?'

'Because,' she said, 'you're not going to be allowed to be with me. No matter what our personal views on the matter might be, you have to think as a king first and a man second. You can't just do what you want.'

'You,' he said with a sigh, 'sound like my grandfather.'

'And he won't think I'm remotely suitable for you. So it's better not to start something we can't finish.'

'What if the barriers were all taken away?' he asked.

If only, she thought. 'And how are you going to do that? There isn't anyone else who can take over from you, is there?'

'No,' he admitted. 'But I think you could be suitable, Indi, if you give yourself a chance.'

'If I change, you mean?'

He shook his head. 'Don't ever change. You're warm and honest and a breath of fresh air. You make things sparkle.'

She stroked his face. 'Lorenzo, don't make this any more difficult than it already is.'

He moved his head so he could press a kiss into her palm. 'You're so stubborn.'

'If the press drag up my past...'

'Then it'll be a two-day wonder, they'll find someone else to gossip about pretty soon after, and nobody's going to judge you on your parents' mistakes.'

'Not just my parents,' she said softly. 'I made a really bad mistake myself.'

Maybe telling him would go some way to making him understand why this couldn't ever work. And it would make him agree with her decision when she found the right words to tell him about the baby.

'Three years ago, my grandfather died.'

'Meaning you were on your own in the world?' Lorenzo asked. 'Well, except your father, and he doesn't count.'

She gave him a wry smile. 'Pretty much, on both counts. Anyway, not long after that I was dragged off to some party. I didn't really want to be there.' She sighed. 'And I met Nigel. He asked me out. I said no, but he was persistent, and I guess... It's weak of me, but...' She stopped, unable to frame the words.

'You were still grieving for someone you loved very much,' Lorenzo said softly. 'It's only natural that you wanted to try and fill some of the hole your grandfather's death had left in your life.'

'I guess.' She stared miserably at the table. 'So I started seeing him. And I was busy sorting out my grandfather's estate and finding a new studio and somewhere else to live, so that kind of distracted me from the things I should've noticed.'

'Why did you have to move?' he asked.

'Because my deal with the earl was that the cottage was my grandparents' for life. After they died, it reverted to him.'

'And he didn't offer to let you stay, at least until you'd found your feet?' Lorenzo looked shocked. 'How mean can you get?'

'That's possibly a bit unfair. I didn't actually give him the chance to offer,' she admitted. 'I moved straight out.'

'Stubborn.'

'Too much so for my own good, sometimes.' She gave him a wry smile. 'So I guess I had enough going on in my life not to notice that Nigel was sometimes a bit cagey when he answered his mobile phone. Or that he only ever visited me—he never invited me back to his place. When we went out, it was always to obscure places—the kind of places I like, because I'd prefer to go somewhere for dinner because the food is amazing rather than because it's trendy. I thought that was why he chose the restaurants.' She shook her head in frustration. 'But I guess he picked them because he wouldn't know anyone there. I never met any of his friends, and he didn't seem interested in meeting mine. It never *occurred* to me that he might be married. I mean, when I look at it now, the signs were all there and it's blindingly obvious, but I was too stupid and naive to read them at the time.'

'It's easy to see things in hindsight. No, you were busy

and you were grieving and you put your trust in the wrong person,' Lorenzo said.

'Yeah.' She couldn't quite bring herself to tell him about the miscarriage. 'Anyway, then I found out he was married. And that he had a baby. He cheated on his wife when she was pregnant, Lorenzo. And he cheated on her with *me*. I can't forgive myself for that.'

He frowned. 'If you'd known he was married, you would've kept turning him down.'

She stared at him. 'Of course I would. I'd seen the damage my mother did. I didn't want to follow in her footsteps.'

'You don't have to tell me that, Indi,' he said softly. 'I already know that you're not your mother.'

'But don't you see? If the press find out...' She bit her lip.

'You met Nigel when you were vulnerable, and he took advantage of that. It isn't your fault.'

'I could have said no.'

'You were grieving and lonely. Anyone else would've done the same, in your shoes.'

'Lorenzo, I've just told you that I had an affair with a married man. Doesn't that...?' She shook her head, frustrated that she couldn't find the right words to make him see her point.

'No, it doesn't make any difference. And if the press does manage to drag it up, then my press team will make sure they're aware of your side of the story to balance things out. You're human, Indi.'

'And you need someone who's perfect.'

'No. Right now,' he said softly, 'I just need you.'

And she could see in his eyes that he meant it.

Even though her common sense knew that this was a huge mistake, how could she push him away when he'd let his barriers down with her like this?

She opened her arms; he held her close, then picked her up and carried her to the sofa in her living room. He settled down with her half lying across his lap. 'Right now,' he whispered, 'I just want to be with you. No talking, no nothing—I just want to *be*.'

That was just fine by her. Back in their bubble, where they had the chance to be together. Warm and comfortable and cosy and...

Indigo had no idea when she fell asleep—or when he did—but she woke when Lorenzo carried her into her bedroom and laid her on the bed, then tucked a duvet round her.

'Lorenzo?' she asked sleepily. 'What time is it?'

'Three in the morning. I'm sorry. I guess I relaxed with you so much that I dozed off,' he said softly. 'I'd better go.'

'You could stay,' she said.

He shook his head. 'I can't. But I'll see you in the morning.' He kissed her lightly. 'I'll take you round the cathedral.'

'And I promise not to be late. Or sleep through the meeting.'

The next morning, Indigo was in Salvatore's office ten minutes before she was due to meet Lorenzo.

'You look up to your eyes in work, Signor Pozzi,' she said.

He shrugged. 'It's a busy time, Signorina Moran. It's the same for everyone.'

'Can I fetch you a cup of coffee or something?' she asked.

He looked at her in surprise. 'Why would you do that?'

'Because you're very busy, and I have ten minutes before His Royal Highness is expecting me, so I have the time to make you some coffee,' she said. 'Do you take milk or sugar?'

'I...' And then he gave her the first real smile she'd seen

since she'd come to the castle. 'Thank you very much. That would be lovely. No milk or sugar, thank you.'

'Just very strong, the way His Royal Highness drinks it?' she asked dryly.

Salvatore spread his hands. 'What can I say?'

'You're from Melvante. Which isn't quite Italian, but pretty near it,' she said with a smile.

She made coffee in the small kitchen next to the office—just about managing not to gag at the scent—and took the mug through to Lorenzo's assistant along with a glass of water. He was on the phone when she got back, so she just placed the mug and glass on a coaster within his reach, and sat quietly in the corner of the office, sketching out some ideas for the window.

Dead on time, Lorenzo came through into his assistant's office. 'Good morning, Signorina Moran. Are you ready to go to the cathedral?'

She put her sketchbook away. 'Of course, Your Royal Highness.'

'You'll like the glass,' Salvatore said. 'Don't let the prince rush you past the rose window.'

'I won't,' she said with a smile.

'What did you do to Salvatore?' Lorenzo asked when they'd left the office.

She shrugged. 'Nothing. Why?'

'Because his job is to be a dragon and protect my time, and there he was telling you not to rush.'

'I made him a mug of coffee, that's all.'

Lorenzo raised an eyebrow. 'I don't think anyone due in a meeting with me has ever done that before.'

'The poor man's up to his eyes, fielding calls and organising things for you. It was the least I could do.'

'Typical you,' Lorenzo said, but his gaze was warm rather than full of censure.

Even from the outside, the cathedral was stunning, all white stone and Gothic arches. Inside, it was even more grand, with soaring arches everywhere and tall, narrow windows—and then a window that made Indigo stop and gasp in pleasure.

'It's beautiful. Like the rose window at York Minster. Why didn't you tell me it was this good?'

He smiled. 'I did tell you to come and see the glass for yourself.' He added softly, 'Remember when you took me to see your angel and the centaur?'

And they'd talked about weddings.

This was where Lorenzo would get married.

Not to her, because she wasn't suitable. But Indigo hoped that Lorenzo would find a royal bride who really loved him—a woman who felt the same way about him that she did.

And then it hit her that she really was in love with him. Bone deep in love with the father of her unborn child. The one man she knew had integrity and she could trust with her heart. Except…they came from different worlds, and she just couldn't see how they'd ever get past that.

'It's beautiful,' she said, forcing herself to focus on the glass.

She enjoyed the rest of the tour of the building, and see-ing the ancient throne on which Lorenzo would be seated during the coronation; but all the time she was aware of the widening gulf between them. Just how was she going to be able to tell him about the baby?

They were walking back down the aisle when a small girl came running towards them, tripped on one of the flagstones and fell flat on her face. Indigo scanned the area quickly but couldn't immediately see anyone who looked like a concerned parent or nanny rushing to the child's aid.

The little girl was crying and holding her knee. Indigo went over to her. 'It's all right, we'll find your mummy for you.'

She was rewarded with a blank stare and more tears.

Of course—the little girl didn't speak English. And Indigo knew that her Italian was too scrappy to be useful right now. 'Lorenzo, can you translate for me?' she asked swiftly. 'Tell her that it's OK, and we'll find her mummy for her.'

The little girl was still crying, but she listened to Lorenzo and nodded.

'I've got something in my bag that will stop her knee feeling sore,' Indigo said, taking the small first aid kit out of her bag and finding the antiseptic wipes and a sticking plaster. 'Can you distract her—get her to find something in one of the windows?'

If Lorenzo had been faced with a crying child on his own, he wouldn't have been quite sure what to do or say. But, with Indigo by his side, it was surprisingly easy. 'It's all right, little one. We'll make your knee better and find your mummy,' he said. 'Can you see all the pretty colours in the windows?'

She nodded.

'What's your favourite colour?' he asked as Indigo wiped her knee clean.

'Pink,' she said, and he couldn't help smiling.

He kept her talking while Indigo ministered to her knee and put a sticking plaster over the cut. They'd just finished when a woman ran up to them.

'Melissa! What happened? Are you all right?' She scooped the little girl into her arms. 'I looked round, and you'd gone.' And then she looked at Lorenzo and did a double-take. 'Your Royal Highness! I'm—oh—um...'

'It's all right,' he said, smiling at her to put her at her

ease. 'Your little girl fell over and cut her knee. My friend's just cleaned the cut and put a sticking plaster on it. I hope that's OK.'

'I—oh, yes, thank you so much. But you're…you're… Your Royal Highness,' she blurted out, clearly still flustered.

'We just did what anyone else would've done,' he said.

'Thank you so much, Your Royal Highness. Melissa, you must always hold Mummy's hand when we're out and never, ever go off without Mummy,' the woman said to her little girl. 'Now, curtsey to the prince and say thank you.'

'Mille grazie,' the little girl said, her lower lip wobbling slightly as she tried to do a graceful curtsey.

'Very nice to meet you, Melissa,' Lorenzo said solemnly.

She looked almost as overawed as her mother.

'I'm afraid I'm expected elsewhere now, but do enjoy the rest of your time here,' Lorenzo said.

'Thank you, Your Royal Highness.'

The woman was about to curtsey, but he placed his hand lightly on her arm. 'You really don't need to curtsey to me.' He smiled. 'Have a nice day.'

'I think you just made a hit,' Indigo said as they left the cathedral.

'Only because you were with me. I wouldn't have had a clue what to say otherwise,' he said.

'You would've improvised,' she said, giving him a cheeky wink. 'And you would've been fine.'

Funny how her belief in him warmed him so much.

All he needed now was to get her to believe in *them*.

Ha. All.

Back at the castle, Lorenzo had a swift conversation with Salvatore, then checked his schedule. 'I'm doing a photo shoot with Indigo for the window, so she can see the state robes,' he said. 'We'll be in my apartment if there's anything urgent, but I'm going to switch my mobile off during the shoot so we don't get constant interruptions.'

'Very good, Your Royal Highness,' Salvatore said. 'Did you enjoy the cathedral, Signorina Moran?'

'I did, Signor Pozzi—the rose window is stunning,' Indigo said. 'And please call me Indi. I prefer being on first-name terms with my clients and their colleagues.'

'Then you shall call me Sal,' he said with a smile.

Lorenzo led her off to his apartment. 'Salvatore has really taken a shine to you,' he said. 'I wish I could make people warm to me so quickly.'

'You can,' she said. 'Just be yourself, and don't put all the formal barriers up.' She wrinkled her nose. 'Though I guess that's easier said than done, when you have to deal with protocol all the time.'

'Protocol,' he said, 'maybe needs to learn to change with the times.'

'Dat's ma boy,' she said with a grin. 'You're learning.'

'Give me ten minutes to change. Be as nosey as you like,' he invited.

'Thank you. I will.'

Lorenzo's apartment was at the opposite end of the castle to hers. It had a view of what looked like a format knot garden; but the interior was lovely, with simple furnishings rather than the ornate Louis XIV tables and chairs she'd seen in the rest of the castle. And she loved the artwork on the walls.

There was a piano in his sitting room, along with a bed for the dog that looked as if it were rarely used—from what she'd seen of Caesar, the spaniel would head straight for the rug in front of the fire or a comfortable corner of the sofa. Bookshelves, containing a mixture of biographies, historical tomes and some very geeky science fiction; no music, she noticed, but knowing Lorenzo his collection was probably digital and centrally organised in a system so that he could access it anywhere in his apartment. There was a television, so obviously he watched the occasional programme, but there were no films on the shelves; she assumed that again he used a digital cloud-based service.

The kitchen was all clean lines. His fridge wasn't that well stocked, so she guessed that most of the time he was served by the palace kitchens rather than cooking for himself. There was a table so he could eat in the kitchen if he wanted to, but this was very much a bachelor apartment, she thought, rather than a family one.

She didn't quite have the nerve to explore his bathroom—a bit too personal, she thought, and his bedroom was definitely out of bounds. He'd made it clear that he wanted to change into his robes without an audience.

The sitting room would be the best place to take the photographs, she decided, when he emerged from his room in a dress uniform with a dark blue floor-length cloak trimmed with gold and ermine.

'Very nice, Your Royal Highness,' she said.

'Hmm. Have a nice snoop, did we?'

'Pretty much. You don't have any cake in your kitchen,' she said, teasing him a little to cover the fact that she felt just a little bit out of her depth. 'And I couldn't find your music or films.'

'They're all cloud-based,' he explained. 'Except the cake. Which is an omission I clearly need to remedy.'

'Uh-huh. Well, let's get this shoot sorted.' It didn't take long for her to get the shots she needed. Or, rather, most of them. 'It won't kill you to smile, you know,' she said.

He gave her a formal smile—one that didn't reach his eyes and made him look totally unreachable.

How could she make him take those barriers down?

She knew it was crazy—totally crazy—but she went with the impulse. She walked over to him, slid her arms round his neck and kissed him.

And then she took a step back. 'Lorenzo,' she said softly.

And he smiled at her.

A real smile, full of warmth. The look she loved most on him, all soft and sweet and touchable.

She took the shot, and he grimaced. 'Do you use that strategy with all your models?'

'I don't usually have models,' she said. But she knew he knew the answer. Of course she didn't. She didn't react to anyone the same way she reacted to Lorenzo.

'You kissed me just to get a photograph.'

He looked thoroughly put out, and she couldn't help smiling. 'Not just to get the photo. I kissed you because right now you look like Prince Hottie. Sexy as hell.'

The light came back into his eyes. 'Put the camera down, Indi.'

'Can't.' She shook her head. 'I'm working.'

'That's a royal command, I'll have you know. Put the camera down.'

She lifted her chin. 'Or what, Your Royal Highness?'

'Or face the consequences.'

She smiled. 'Bring it on, Lorenzo.'

'You asked for it,' he said, and took the camera gently from her hand, placing it safely out of the way. And then he kissed her until her knees were on the point of buckling.

'That has consequences, too, you know,' she said, and undid the clasp of his robe before sliding it off his shoulders. She folded it neatly and placed it over the back of the chair.

'Interesting,' he commented, but his voice was full of warmth. 'You've turned into a neat freak, Indi.'

'No chance.' She spread her hands. 'But this is your coronation robe. I don't want you to get into trouble with your wardrobe people.'

He laughed. 'This is the twenty-first century. It's not how things were a hundred years ago, when people with titles still employed valets and ladies' maids.'

'Even so, I don't want to crumple your robes.' She stroked them, enjoying the softness under her fingertips. 'I have to say, Your Royal Highness, you look mighty fine in navy.' She looked at him. 'And even better without your robes.'

'Was that a hint?' He stripped out of his uniform, laying it neatly on top of his robes, and maintaining eye contact with her the entire time. By the time he'd stripped down to his underwear, Indigo felt as if she was about to spontaneously combust.

And then he simply picked her up and carried her into his bedroom. When he set her down on her feet again, he made sure that her body was in close contact to his, so she was left fully aware of how much he wanted her. And then he proceeded to make love to her until she felt as if her bones had melted.

Later, lying curled in his arms, Indigo thought how this was every bit as good as their time spent in England. The physical attraction between them was still strong.

But would it be enough to help them keep the world at bay?

And how would he cope when she told him her news?

'Penny for them?' he asked, stroking her hair away from his forehead.

No. Now wasn't the right time. 'Just worrying that I've made you late for something.'

He glanced at his watch. 'Um.'

'Sorry. You're going to be up to your eyes, now.'

'Yes,' he said regretfully, and switched on his phone. Immediately his phone started beeping with a barrage of incoming messages.

'Go and do whatever you need to do,' she said, 'and I'll sort things out here.'

'Are you sure?'

'I'm sure,' she confirmed. 'Go and do all your prince stuff.'

'You're wonderful.' He dressed swiftly, kissed her again, and vanished. She took her time, and made sure she hung up his uniform and his robes properly before putting his bed to rights, then took her work things back to her apartment and went back to sketching out designs.

Later that afternoon, Lorenzo came by her apartment. 'We forgot the crown.'

She raised an eyebrow. 'Aren't you supposed to be in a meeting?'

'I can afford to be spontaneous,' he said.

Hmm. She remembered just how spontaneous he'd been in his apartment, and warmth spread through her. 'So where do I get to see you model the crown?' she asked.

'In the vaults. Bring your camera.' He waved a key at her.

She laughed. 'You're telling me that, in this day and age, you're using old-fashioned technology?'

'A little more than that. There are layers.' He took her hand as they walked down the corridor. Even though Indigo was pretty sure that it was going to cause a mad rush of gossip once it was spotted on the palace CCTV, she couldn't quite bring herself to pull away. It felt good, having her fingers tangled with Lorenzo's. She'd loved walking hand in hand with him in the gardens at Edensfield, and this wasn't so very different.

To get to the vaults, they had to pass through a series of doors and use a series of different things to unlock them—codes, fingerprints and even iris recognition.

'I take it back. You're in full James Bond mode,' she teased.

'Which means I get to dally with the beautiful girl.' He stole a kiss, shocking her.

'Lorenzo—was that just caught on CCTV?'

'Probably.'

'But...'

'I don't care. And, for someone who's supposed to be a free spirit, you worry far too much,' Lorenzo said and kissed her again.

Inside the vaults, he took out a box and unlocked it.

'Oh, my.' Indigo had never seen so many jewels in one place—or such large ones.

He took the crown out of the box. 'I can remember my grandfather placing this on my head.'

'When you were little—like dressing up?' she asked.

He shook his head. 'When I was eighteen. I'd just spent a week going off the rails, and he wanted me to understand that I had a commitment. That I needed to—well, strengthen myself so I could carry the burden.' He handed her the crown.

'It's really heavy,' she said, shocked and also a little afraid of dropping it and denting it.

She handed it back to him. 'So why did you go off the rails?'

He was silent for a long, long time. And then he sighed. 'I'm going to tell you something now that maybe half a dozen people know, and they're all sworn to secrecy. Everyone thought my parents died in a car accident when I was ten. But it wasn't an accident.' He blew out a breath. 'My mother was having an affair. She was planning to leave my father, and my father found out. He drove their car into a wall with her beside him, deliberately, because he couldn't bear to be without her and he couldn't bear the idea of her being with anyone else. My grandparents told everyone that it was a tragic accident—but then I found some papers when I was eighteen. Papers that my grandfather had thought were destroyed. And that's when I learned the truth.'

Indigo looked at him, shocked. 'Your father killed himself and your mother? But that meant he'd be leaving you on your own. How—' She shook her head, completely not understanding. 'How could he do that?'

'It's not a choice that I would make,' Lorenzo said. 'If I married someone who hated the world I lived in, I'd find a compromise.'

Was this his way of telling her that that was what he was trying to do, right now? Find a compromise so they could be together?

'I'd love my wife enough to let her go, if I had to. I'd want her to be happy. And if that meant not being with me—well, so be it. I wouldn't stop her,' Lorenzo said. 'But I'd try my hardest to find a way round it, so we could be together.'

She stroked his face. 'And the accident—' she couldn't bear to think of what it really was '—happened not long before you were sent away to school. That's so hard, Lorenzo.' And she could understand now why he'd been brought up in such a rigid, formal way. His grandparents had tried to protect him from the truth.

'I've had a long time to get used to it,' he said softly. 'Take the pictures, Indi. I wasn't intending to be maudlin. I just wanted you to understand.'

'I do. And I promise you it won't go any further than me. Ever.' She kissed him swiftly on the lips. 'And I get now why you keep everyone at a distance. It stops you getting hurt. But if you let people close, Lorenzo—the whole world will love you.' Just as she loved him.

Perhaps, he thought. But there was only one person he wanted to love him.

And he thought that maybe, just maybe, she might feel the same way about him as he felt about her.

But would they be able to find a compromise so she could feel comfortable in his world?

He placed the crown on his head. 'OK. Do what you need to for the designs.'

She took several photographs. And then he placed the crown back in the box, locked it again, and returned it to its place in the vault.

CHAPTER THIRTEEN

THE NEXT DAY, there was a story in the newspapers about the Prince of Hearts, with a photograph of Lorenzo and another of the little girl they'd rescued in the cathedral, standing with her mother.

'I've never had anything like this before,' Lorenzo said, handing her a translated version of the story on a tablet. 'People have always seen me as—well, a bit remote.'

'Low-key's fine. But let them get to know you,' she said, 'and they'll see you're not in the slightest bit remote.'

She scanned through the text. 'Oh, no. They're talking about a mystery woman being with you.' She swallowed hard. 'That means they're going to dig up what they can about me.' Panic flooded through her.

'Stop worrying. For now, the press office will handle it. They'll explain that you're a glass specialist and I was briefing you in the cathedral.'

'But what if…?'

He kissed the tip of her nose. 'Then I'll deal with it. I promise you, there's nothing to worry about.' His voice was very calm. 'And I don't break my promises, Indi. I don't tell lies.'

Whereas she was telling him a lie, sort of. A lie of omission. She was going to have to tell him the truth, very soon. She just needed to work out how.

* * *

He took her through to the palace gardens, that morning. What she'd thought was a formal knot garden turned out to be a series of concentric circles made from stone slabs.

'What's this—some kind of sculpture?' she asked.

'A water maze. If you stand on the wrong slab, it tilts and you get sprayed.'

How come a stuffy, formal palace would have something as crazy and fun as this in the garden?

The question must have been written all over her face, because he said, 'It was my grandmother's idea. She grew up in a house with a hedge maze and she liked the idea of having something fun in the garden. I remember when I was small, I loved the mazes here. I used to spend all day playing here and in the hedge maze.' He looked slightly wistful. 'Life was a bit simpler, back then.'

Before his parents had died? Or before he'd realised what being king would mean?

'OK. So the idea is that you reach the middle without getting wet.' He spread his hands. 'Your challenge, should you wish to accept it…'

'But what,' she asked, 'is my reward, should I beat the challenge?'

He leaned forward. 'Spontaneous inventiveness on my part.'

And, oh, the picture that put in her head.

'You're on,' she said, and picked her way through the first ring.

'Four more to go,' he said.

One and a half rings later, she stepped on the wrong stone. It tilted, and a fountain of water sprayed over her.

She just laughed. 'When you were a kid, I bet you jumped on every stone to make sure you got soaked every single time.'

'I might've done,' he said with a grin.

'Which makes you the expert on how to do it without getting wet, because you know where the tilting slabs are. Show me how it's done,' she said.

He picked his way round the circles until he reached her, then took her hand and showed her which stones to leap over.

Until they were about to reach the centre of the maze, and she jumped on the slab that he was clearly about to avoid. Water sprayed up and over him. 'Gotcha,' she said, laughing.

He laughed back, and jumped onto the same stone, pulling her into his arms at the same time so that the water sprayed over both of them. And while the droplets were still falling, he kissed her stupid.

This was the Lorenzo she'd fallen in love with back at Edensfield. The Lorenzo who'd dressed up in Regency clothing and copied the Mr Darcy scene from the movie, just for her. The Lorenzo who'd carried a tired, elderly dog home through the gardens.

'Lorenzo,' she whispered.

Now was the right time to tell him. When they were laughing in his garden, enjoying some harmless fun. When he was reliving some of the fun of his own childhood. When he could see how it might be for his own child. He'd told her his deepest, darkest secret in the castle vault; and now it was time for her to tell him the truth about the baby.

'Indi.' He kissed her again, and she could see the passion in his eyes.

'There's something I—'

Her words were cut off by his phone shrilling.

He made a nose of frustration. 'Sorry. I'm expecting this.'

And he'd already taken time out to spend with her. Time

he couldn't really afford. 'Go,' she said. 'Is it OK for me to walk in the gardens for a bit longer?'

'Sure. Go where you like. I'll see you later.' He kissed her again, then took the call.

Indigo went back to her room for her camera and sketch-book, then headed out to find the rose garden. Up close, she might get the last ideas she needed for the window design.

And, up close, it was even better than she'd hoped. She closed her eyes and breathed in the scent. The essence of summer, she thought.

Then she became aware of someone speaking to her in rapid Italian. She opened her eyes to see an elderly man carrying secateurs. He was probably one of the palace gardeners, she thought, and he probably thought she was a trespasser.

She dredged up her limited Italian. 'Um, *mi scusi— parla inglese*?'

The man smiled. 'Yes, I speak English.'

And very well, too, she thought; he had only the slight-est trace of an accent.

'Can I help you? Are you lost?' he asked.

How ironic that she'd met Lorenzo at her best friend's house and he'd thought she was a trespasser—and now she was in Lorenzo's home and being mistaken for a tres-passer again.

'I'm not trespassing,' she said hastily, 'I'm working on some designs for a glass window for the palace, and I wanted a closer look at the roses—is that all right?'

'Of course, *signorina*.' He paused. 'May I ask, why the roses?'

'Because they're beautiful and they remind me of home,' she said wistfully. 'My grandparents had a rose garden—nothing on the scale of this, of course, but I love the scent of roses. And I saw the garden from the library window the other day. It's like a rainbow of roses, with the way the colours shade from white to yellow to peach, pink and red. How could I resist coming to see them?'

He looked pleased. 'You like our roses here at the palace?'

She nodded. 'And I like that they're not all the same type—you have floribundas here, mixed with hybrid teas and Bourbons and ramblers.'

He inclined his head. 'So you know your roses.'

'I'm not an expert, by any means,' she said, 'but I know what I like.'

'You grow them yourself?'

She shook her head. 'I only have a windowsill in my flat, so I have a couple of pots of miniature roses. But if I ever move to a place with a garden, I'll have a bower of roses just like we used to have at home.' She smiled back at him and held her hand out for him to shake. 'Sorry, I've been very rude—I should have introduced myself. I'm Indigo Moran.'

'Enzo,' he returned. 'You have a very pretty name.'

'Thank you.'

'Would you like me to show you round?'

'If that's not going to interfere with your job or make you late for something, then yes, please, Enzo. That would be really kind of you.'

She spent the next half hour wandering through the garden with him, learning about the oldest roses in the garden and taking some photographs. 'I really love this one. It's so pretty,' she said, pointing out a crimson rose with pink and white stripes. She leaned over. 'Oh, and the scent's amazing.'

'*Rosa mundi*,' he said. 'It's one of the oldest striped roses known, nearly a thousand years old.'

'It's beautiful,' she said.

'It was the favourite rose of my wife,' he said quietly.

'Oh, I'm sorry—I didn't mean to bring up something that would hurt you.' In impulse, she took his hand and squeezed it.

'They're good memories,' he said. He glanced at her sketchbook. 'May I see?'

'They're just scraps of ideas,' she said.

He flicked through it until he came to a sketch of Lorenzo. 'The young prince.'

'Yes—it's one of the ideas I'm working on.'

'So you've met the prince?'

She nodded. 'Actually, his best friend is the brother of my best friend. He came to stay with them while I was restoring their mermaid window. He liked my work and asked if I would do some designs for a window.'

'For the coronation?' Enzo asked.

'Yes, so I want to make sure I get it right and come up with a design to do him justice. He's a good man and I think he'll make an excellent king.' She grimaced. 'Sorry, I'm not from Melvante and it isn't my place to comment. I don't mean to be rude.'

'But you say things how you see them.'

'Honesty,' Indigo said, 'is always the best policy. Then everyone knows where they are.' She smiled. 'Which isn't an excuse for being rude. You can still be tactful and kind.'

'True.'

They chatted for a bit longer, then Enzo cut half a dozen of the *rosa mundi* roses and gave them to her.

She gasped. 'Is this going to get you into trouble with the king?'

'No. I'm the head gardener, so I can cut any roses I choose,' he said. 'If anyone asks you, say Enzo gave them to you and you're using them to help design your window.'

'I will—and thank you for being so kind and spending so much time with me. *Mille, mille grazie*,' she added.

'My pleasure, child,' he said with a smile, seeming touched that she'd bothered thanking him in his own language.

That evening, it never seemed to be the right time for Indigo to tell Lorenzo what she'd tried to tell him at the water maze. And, the next morning, she had an email from Lottie telling her that she needed to look at the newspapers.

When she did, she discovered a buzz of media speculation. A paparazzo had managed to capture a photograph of her with Lorenzo in the water maze, her hand on his arm, with them looking at each other. And they both looked as if they'd just been thoroughly kissed.

Is our prince falling in love?

Oh, no. She tried to get hold of Lorenzo, but his phone was switched off. In the end, she went to the office to talk to Salvatore. 'When His Royal Highness is free, please can you apologise to him for me?'

'About the papers this morning, you mean?' Salvatore asked.

She nodded. 'That wasn't meant to happen.'

To her relief, he didn't look angry. 'There's nothing you can do about the media, Indi. And it wasn't just you in the photograph, remember. Don't worry. The press office will handle it.'

'They already have enough on their plates, with the coronation.' And she dreaded to think of the media reaction to the rest of the news. A baby, and definitely no wedding because she wasn't a suitable princess.

'You look out of sorts,' Salvatore said, 'and would I be right in thinking it's not just the press?'

She sighed. 'I can't get the design for the window right.

I need to do something with my hands. Normally I'd make something in glass so I can let my subconscious work on whatever's blocking me, but I don't have my tools with me. This visit was just to look at the site and present some designs to His Majesty and His Royal Highness.'

'My sister always makes cake when she wants to think,' he said.

'Making cake would work for me. Or cookies.' She wrinkled her nose. 'Except I don't have a proper kitchen in the apartment.'

'You know we have a little kitchen here in the office. You could use that. And I'll arrange that you can borrow whatever you need from the palace kitchen.'

'And in return you get cookies?' she asked with a smile. 'Sal, thank you, that would be wonderful.'

He made a swift call, then smiled at her. 'Go and see Tonia in the kitchen and she'll get you what you need.'

'You,' she said, 'are a wonderful man.' She kissed his cheek, making him blush; then she headed to the palace kitchen and spoke to Tonia to sort out what she needed, carried the lot back to the office kitchen, and lost herself making shortbread biscuits.

She'd just melted some chocolate ready to decorate the top of the shortbread when Lorenzo walked in. 'What's this, commandeering my office kitchen?'

'Yes.'

'I love the smell of vanilla.' He stole one of the warm biscuits and tasted it. 'Mmm. This is good.'

She tapped the back of his hand. 'I don't know about Prince of Hearts—I think you're the knave, stealing shortbread.'

'The knave of hearts,' he said, 'allegedly stole tarts, not shortbread.'

'Same difference.'

He laughed. 'I never get told off in the palace kitchen.'

'Really? Well, you're getting told off in mine.' On impulse, she dipped her finger into the melted chocolate and dabbed a stripe on each cheek.

He looked at her. 'That's war paint. Hmm. Now there's an idea.' He dipped his finger into the melted chocolate, too.

As soon as Indigo realised his intentions, she ran.

Too late. He caught her, and painted her lips with the melted chocolate. And then he kissed it off.

Very, *very* slowly.

'I give in,' she sighed.

'Good.' He paused. 'So why are you baking?'

'I needed time to think about my design—I'm stuck on something, and my subconscious needs to work through it,' she said. She grimaced. 'And then there's that bit in the paper. I'm so sorry.'

'The photograph.' He didn't look in the slightest bit fazed. 'Yes, the press office has been fielding calls all morning.' He shrugged. 'Maybe it's better out in the open.'

'But you—we—we *can't*. You're supposed to marry a princess.'

'This is the twenty-first century. And, apart from the fact that I can marry someone not of royal blood if I choose, you're the daughter of an earl.'

'Illegitimate daughter,' she corrected. 'And my past is messy.' She still hadn't told him quite all of it. Or about their baby. But, the longer she left it, the harder it became, and she didn't want to just blurt it out.

'You're human,' he said. 'And people like you.' He tipped his head slightly to one side. 'People like the man I am, when I'm with you. *I* like the man I am, when I'm with you.'

'But it's not just you. There's your grandfather,' she said.

'I have a feeling he's going to like you.'

'But it's not enough,' she said. 'You have your position to think of.'

He grinned. 'Which is, right now, in my office kitchen, covered in crumbs and with chocolate all over my face. Very princely.'

'Lorenzo, why are you making it so hard?' she asked.

'I'm not,' he said softly. 'From where I'm standing, it's easy. You just have to believe. In *yourself*, as well as in us.'

That, she thought, was the rub. She couldn't believe in them until she believed in herself. And how could she possibly see herself as the wife of a king, having to live up to so many expectations when she'd been found so wanting in the past?

'I believe in you. And in us,' he said softly, and kissed her again. 'I'm stuck in official stuff all evening. But I'll see you tomorrow. We'll talk then.'

And she'd have to tell him then, she thought. She'd really, really have to tell him. She couldn't put it off any longer.

Predictably, Lorenzo was caught up in palace business until just before the time when he was due to introduce Indigo to his grandfather for the presentation of her designs, on the morning of the charity ball.

'Sorry,' he said, and kissed her on the cheek.

'It can't be helped. I know you're busy,' she said. Though inwardly she wondered: just supposing they did manage to make a go of things between them, would he be able to carve out enough time to spend with their baby?

Not that she could ask.

He ushered her in to one of the state rooms. And Indigo froze in horror when she saw the man sitting at the head of the table: the man she chatted to in the garden. She nearly dropped her laptop.

'I—you're Lorenzo's grandfather?' she asked, staring at him.

Lorenzo frowned. 'What's going on? Nonno? Indi?'

'We met in the rose garden, the other day,' Enzo explained. 'I was a little…mendacious, perhaps.'

A little? He could say that again. 'I thought there was something familiar about you, but I told myself I was just being ridiculous,' Indigo said.

Enzo shrugged. 'And when you see an elderly man wearing sensible clothes for gardening, you don't expect him to be the king.'

Even though, she thought, Lorenzo had pretty much warned her back in England. Hadn't he said that he would know exactly where to find his grandfather after he retired—in the rose garden? She really should have thought a little harder.

'You told me you were the head gardener,' she said, forgetting all about protocol and the correct method of addressing the King of Melvante.

'Strictly speaking, I am,' Enzo said.

Indigo blew out a breath. 'Well, I apologise if I was rude or said anything out of line. Your Majesty,' she added belatedly.

'I think,' Lorenzo said, 'Nonno was just as much in the wrong as you were. More so, in fact, because he misled you. And you probably weren't rude.'

'She wasn't. Though she does believe in plain speaking,' Enzo said. 'Which is refreshing. Now, Signorina Moran—Indigo—would you like to show us your designs officially?'

'You saw the rough sketches,' Indigo said. 'These are the proper proposals, Your Majesty. I hope you'll allow me to talk you through my ideas.'

* * *

Lorenzo sat back and watched as Indigo went into professional mode. She had a presentation on her laptop which she'd clearly run through a few times because her words were flawless. Then she gave them both paper copies so they could take a closer look; and she'd also made a rough copy of some of her designs on tracing paper and held it up to the window so they could see the colours.

'So the roses aren't a prison, this time,' Enzo said.

Colour flared in Indigo's cheeks. 'You saw the drawing?'

'It was why I agreed to the commission,' Enzo said. 'I notice my grandson isn't an angel this time.'

'He can hardly be an angel at his coronation,' she pointed out.

He looked more closely at one of the designs. 'Is that Caesar at his feet?'

'Um, yes,' she said. 'I could make the window without the dog, if you prefer. But I thought it might be a nice touch to make Lorenzo seem more human.'

Lorenzo coughed. 'I am still here, you know.'

'I know.' She smiled at him, her expression all warm and soft and sweet. 'Lorenzo, having your dog with you is something your people will be able to relate to—a beloved pet. It'll make them feel closer to you.'

'Good point,' Enzo said, sounding approving. 'I vote to keep him. And I like this one, very much. You've captured something in my grandson, Indigo. Something I never expected to see.' This time, he met Lorenzo's gaze. 'But I'm glad it's there.'

Lorenzo knew exactly what his grandfather was saying, and relief flooded through him. Now all he had to do was convince Indigo.

Once they'd finished their discussion, she curtseyed and left the room.

'Thank you,' Lorenzo said quietly, and hugged his grandfather.

Enzo raised an eyebrow. 'She's changed you. And it's a good change.'

'I need to talk to her.'

'Go, child. With my blessing,' Enzo said softly.

Lorenzo caught up with Indigo just outside her apartment. 'Are you OK?'

'Yes.' She sucked in a breath. 'Just a bit shocked that the man I was chatting to in the garden turned out to be your grandfather. I must've broken all kinds of protocol.'

'Sometimes protocol needs to be broken—and, if you think about it, he broke it as much as you did.' He paused. 'He's on our side, Indi.' When she didn't look convinced, he leaned forward and brushed his mouth against hers. 'Trust me,' he said softly.

That was the rub, Indigo thought. She wanted to trust him. She knew he was an honourable man. But that made everything even more mixed up and harder to say. 'You must have a million and one things to do.'

'I can postpone them, if you need me to.'

No. She was never, ever going to stand in the way of what he had to do for his country. 'I'm fine. I need to work out the glass order for your window. Go and do princely stuff.'

He smiled. 'I'll see you at the ball tonight.'

And then—then, she would definitely tell him. After the ball. 'See you later,' she said, and forced herself to smile as sweetly as she could.

CHAPTER FOURTEEN

IT TOOK INDIGO the second half of the afternoon to get ready for the ball. Lottie's gown was gorgeous—plain black and strapless, with a frothy ankle-length skirt that reminded Indigo of a ballerina's dress. And Lottie had given her an early birthday present to go with the dress—an enamelled pendant in the shape of a butterfly, coloured iridescent green and blue. That was the only jewellery she wore.

She didn't look in the slightest bit like a princess, she thought as she looked in the mirror. She looked like a little girl playing dress-up. This wasn't who she was—but it was who she'd have to be in Lorenzo's world.

He'd said that he liked the man he was when she was with him.

Could she learn to like the woman she'd have to be, by his side?

She shook herself, and marched down to the ballroom—luckily Salvatore had given her directions earlier. Salvatore was at the door of the ballroom, and smiled when he saw her. 'You look enchanting, Indi.'

'*Grazie*, Sal.' Even if he was just being polite and flattering, she'd take it. Because right now she could feel every bit of adrenalin running through her veins and spiralling into panic.

'Let me introduce you to some people.' With relief, she noticed that he introduced her as a professional glass expert. And everyone spoke English, so her limited Italian wasn't stretched too far.

Even so, she was aware of people watching her and she knew they were speculating about the photographs and stories in the press. Who was Indigo Moran—Cinderella, or a gold-digger out for what she could get?

It was worse when Lorenzo walked in, because everyone was watching both of them. And either he wasn't aware of it or he was trying to make a point, because he came straight over to her. 'Come and dance with me?'

'I—haven't you got loads of meeting and greeting to do?' she asked, panicking.

'It's a ball. People are supposed to dance at balls, Indi,' he teased.

'Proper ballroom dancing. I've never done this sort of thing. I'm going to trip over and fall flat on my face.'

'Not if your partner knows how to lead you properly,' he reassured her.

For one horrified moment, she thought he was going to kiss her. *In public.* But, to her relief, he simply smiled. And then he swept her into his arms.

'All you have to do is remember to use alternate legs, and go where I steer you,' he said softly as the waltz began.

She discovered that he was absolutely right. In his arms, and with him guiding her, she couldn't fall and make an idiot of herself. And she found herself relaxing, enjoying being in his arms.

He danced with her twice more during the evening. So did Salvatore, as if he realised she was feeling just a bit unsure of herself and could do with some back-up.

But then she went to the Ladies'. She was adjusting her dress when she heard people talking.

'She's plainer than I thought she'd be,' someone said.

In English. Indigo's skin crawled. Did they know she was here and meant her to overhear every word? Or were they just gossiping and at least one person in the group didn't speak good Italian so they were speaking in English to keep her in the loop?

'Darling, she must have something—the prince seems besotted with her.' This voice was more heavily accented.

'But he can't marry her, surely? She's not blue-blooded,' someone else said.

'She's definitely got her eye on the crown. Lorenzo's easy on the eye, but he's so reserved. He'd be such hard work as a husband. But I guess if you want money, you don't care about that sort of thing.'

Indigo was livid that these women had got Lorenzo so wrong and were being so mean about him. But she also knew that if she stormed out of the cubicle and put them straight, they wouldn't believe her—because they'd already decided that she was a gold-digger and her word wouldn't be accepted

She wouldn't be acceptable as Lorenzo's partner, either.

And although she knew he'd be gallant and fight her corner for her, it would place their relationship under such a strain.

He'd said that he wouldn't be like his father; if the woman he loved was unhappy in his world, he'd let her go because he wanted her to be happy. So now she needed to do exactly the same for him—to let him go, so he could find someone that the world would deem a suitable bride for him and let him be happy.

She stayed in her cubicle until the gossiping women had gone—not because she was a coward and afraid to face them, but because she knew that nothing she said would make a difference so it would be a waste of time and effort to confront them—and then slipped back out into the ballroom and found Salvatore.

'I've got a bit of a headache,' she said. 'I think I'm going to have an early night.'

'Can I get you some painkillers?' he asked.

She shook her head. 'That's really sweet of you, Sal, but a bit of sleep's the best thing for me.' Not that she'd be able to sleep. It'd be another night of lying awake at two a.m., worrying and wondering just how she was going to fix things. 'Can you give my apologies to whoever needs them, please?'

'Of course. Would you like me to walk you back to your apartment?'

'Thanks, but you don't have to do that. Really. I'll be fine.' She kissed his cheek. 'I'll see you later.'

As she headed back to her apartment, her heart was breaking.

She was doing the right thing—she *knew* she was—but why did it have to hurt so much?

Tomorrow morning, she'd tell Lorenzo about the baby, and then she'd get a flight back to England. She could work on the window over there and ship it over to Melvante when it was finished. And maybe they could time it so Lorenzo was away from the palace when she came to put the window in place.

'Where's Indi?' Lorenzo asked Salvatore. 'I can't see her anywhere.'

'She had a headache. She's gone back to her apartment for an early night,' his assistant said.

'Hmm.' Lorenzo frowned. 'Something's wrong.'

'Maybe the ball's a little overwhelming.'

Lorenzo shook his head. 'There's more to it than that. I've got a funny feeling. Cover for me, will you?'

'Are you sure about this?' Salvatore asked.

'More sure than I've been about anything,' Lorenzo said, and left the ballroom.

When he knocked on Indigo's door, she took a while to answer. She'd changed out of the ball gown into jeans and a T-shirt; with no make-up on and her hair pulled back, she looked young and very vulnerable.

'How are you feeling?' he asked.

'I'm OK,' she said, and he knew she was lying. 'You shouldn't be here. You're supposed to be at the ball.'

'You disappeared,' he said.

'I have a headache. An early night will sort me out.'

But he could see through the open door to her bedroom—and to the suitcase on the bed, half packed. 'Indi, I think we need to talk.'

'I...' She sighed and stood aside to let him in.

'Are you planning to leave?' he asked when he'd closed the door behind him.

'Tomorrow. I've finished the design. I'll go back and make the window.'

'Can't you make it here?' he asked.

'Better not.'

He frowned. 'What about us?'

'There can't be an us,' she said softly. 'Lorenzo—sit down. I need to talk to you about something.'

He frowned, but did as she asked and sat on the sofa.

Instead of sitting next to him, she sat on the arm of the chair furthest from him. 'I've been trying to find the right words to tell you, but I can't, so I'm going to have to be blunt about it.' She swallowed hard. 'I'm pregnant.'

'You're...' He couldn't quite take this in. 'How long?'

'About nine weeks.'

'How long have you known?'

'A couple of weeks. I've had a dating scan at the hospital.'

'Why didn't you tell me before?'

'Because I couldn't find the right words—or the right time.'

That was fair comment. He'd been rushing around all over the place and hadn't spent much time with her. Though there had been moments when they'd been close. Why hadn't she trusted him with the news then?

He blew out a breath. 'OK. We'll get married.'

'We will *not*,' she corrected.

'Indi, you're expecting my baby. What do you think I'm going to do, abandon you?'

She flinched.

Which wasn't so surprising. She'd been abandoned by her parents, and then dumped by a man who'd cheated on his wife with her.

'It's kind of traditional in my family to get married before you have a baby,' he said, hoping that he sounded light and gentle enough to ease her worries.

Her face was set. 'That's not going to work, and you know it. We've already talked about why we can't be together. Marriage is *that*—' she gestured wildly '—multiplied by a hundred.'

'We need to talk about this, Indi.' He moved to take her hand, but she pulled away. Hurt, he stared at her. 'Indi?'

'Just—please don't touch me. I need to keep a clear head,' she whispered.

That had to be the most backhanded compliment ever: she didn't want him to touch her because she didn't trust herself to think straight if he held her hand. Or did she not trust him not to bully her? He damped down his feelings. 'OK. Let's cut to the chase. You're expecting my child. Of course I want to be there and support you. And the best way for me to do that is if you marry me.'

'Because a king-to-be can't possibly have an illegitimate child?' she asked.

'I don't want to marry you out of duty or to satisfy any social conventions, if that's what you're thinking.' He blew out a breath. 'Right now, you're upset and you're worried. I don't think you'll believe me if I tell you how I feel about you.' He looked her straight in the eye. 'But I'm going to tell you anyway. I fell in love with you, back in Edensfield. You're a breath of fresh air, Indi. My world's a much better place when you're in it. And I'd like you there permanently. You and our child.'

'That picture I drew for you—did you look at it?' she asked. '*Really* look at it?'

'The prince in a bower of roses. Except the roses don't quite hide the fact that he's actually in a cage. Yes, I noticed,' he said dryly.

'That's your life, Lorenzo. It was what you were born to and you're accustomed to it. But I don't want that kind of life for our child,' she said. 'I don't care how gilded the cage might be, it's still a cage. Our baby won't have the freedom to make mistakes and learn from them.'

'So what's the alternative? Freedom, but not having his or her parents together? Not being part of a family?'

She flinched. 'Plenty of people grow up in single-parent families, and they're just fine. They're still loved and the parent they live with gives their best.'

'You and I,' he said, 'were both brought up by our grandparents. Both of us were sent away to school. I think, if we're both honest about it, we were lonely and we felt pretty much a burden to our grandparents. And I don't want that for my child. I want to live with my child. I want to be there for the first smile and the first tooth and the first word and the first step. I want my child to be part of a family. With *me*.'

Her eyes widened. 'Are you saying you'll fight me for custody?'

'No.' He raked a hand through her hair. 'What kind of monster do you think I am? I'm saying I want to do all that with you *and* our baby. Yes, you're right, as my consort you won't have the kind of freedom you've been used to in your life so far. You'll have a security team and a schedule. But there's room for compromise.'

'Is there? Because it seems as if I'm the one giving up everything.'

'You don't have to give up your friends or your job,' he said. 'OK, I admit, you won't be able to do your work to quite the same extent that you do now, because sometimes I'll need you to support me in state affairs and that means attending functions with me. But you don't have to give it up completely. It's important that you have your own interests.'

She still didn't look convinced.

'I want you in my life, Indi,' he said softly. 'Not because you're carrying my child, and not because I think this is the quick way to get everything a king is supposed to have—a crown, a queen and an heir. I want you for *you*.' He paused. 'You've talked about what you have to give up, but have you thought about what you'd gain if you married me?'

'Marriage to a king, and an unlimited budget. Social status and money might be what some people would want—and it's what people think I want.'

'What people?'

She swallowed hard. 'In the Ladies'. I heard them talking about me. They think I'm after a crown.'

He snorted. 'Like hell you are. That's not what you're about, and if they're too narrow-minded to see that then it's their problem.' He shook his head. 'And, actually, it's not what I meant. I think we can give each other something that neither of us has ever really had. We'll both be the centre of our family, not a burden tagging round the edges. Not someone who's going to be sent away.'

For a second, he saw longing in her eyes. He was pretty sure she wanted this, deep down, just as much as he did. But he knew that if he pushed her too hard, too fast, he'd drive her away. She had to come to terms with her own demons, the things that stopped her from wanting to be with him. Maybe she'd come to trust him enough to help her, but at the end of the day the only person who could really fight her fears was Indigo herself.

'At Edensfield,' he said, 'I asked you to make our relationship permanent. I gave you a choice. I knew what I wanted—just as I know what I want now—but I'm not going to bully you into choosing that. I want you to be with me because you want to be here. I don't want you to stay because you think you ought to for our child's sake or because you feel pressured. I want you to stay because you love me and you want to be with me, the way I want to be with you.'

She bit her lip. 'But how can I ever be acceptable in your world? How, with my past?'

'Everyone makes mistakes. The trick is to learn from them and not repeat them.' He sighed. 'Indi, you're hiding behind an excuse.'

She glowered at him. 'No, I'm not.'

'If I wasn't the heir to Melvante and I asked you to marry me, would it be different?'

She was silent for a long time. Then she sighed. 'Yes.'

'And that's the rub,' he said. 'I can't be someone I'm not, Indi. I'm an only child and so was my father. There's nobody else to take over from me. If I abdicate, so I can be the ordinary man you want, then I'd be letting my family down and I'd be letting my country down. But if I don't abdicate, I don't have you. Either way, I lose.' He looked at her. 'Unless you can be brave enough to believe in yourself and take me for who I am.'

'I'm not sure if I'm brave enough,' she said, biting her lip. 'I'm scared that it's all going to go wrong.'

'You're scared that I'll let you down, the way Nigel did? I'm not your ex, Indi.'

'No. You're an honourable man. You didn't even question whether the baby was yours.'

'Why on earth would I? Of course the baby's mine.' He frowned. 'Did *he* do that?'

She nodded. 'And he wanted me to have a termination.' She dragged in a breath. 'He said he already had one brat and he didn't want another.'

'That's despicable,' Lorenzo said. 'I want him in a boxing ring with me. Right now.'

She shook her head. 'Violence doesn't solve anything.'

'I know, but it'd be very satisfying to bring him to his knees and make him grovel to you.'

'I don't care about Nigel. I stopped loving him when I realised what a louse he was,' she said.

'Good. Because I'd hate to think he could hurt you again.' He stroked her face. 'Indi. I'm not him. I'm not going to abandon you—or our baby. And I'm certainly not going to ask you to have a termination.'

'I lost the baby. At thirteen weeks, I had a miscarriage. I'd already had a scan. I'd seen my baby's heart beating. And I...I...' She looked away.

Lorenzo stood up and went over to her, scooped her up in his arms and sat down, settling her in his lap with his arms wrapped tightly round her. 'I'm so sorry you had to go through all that. And on your own.'

'I wasn't on my own. Lottie held my hand all the way.'

'I'm glad.'

'She nearly missed Gus's wedding. I said she had to go because she was a bridesmaid, and I'd be fine on my own.'

'So that's why I didn't meet you at Gus's wedding. I was the best man,' he said. He kissed her hair. 'I'm sorry you lost the baby. That must've been hard for you. But, Indi, having a miscarriage in the past doesn't mean that you're going to lose our baby this time round.'

'I know. At least, the sensible bit of me knows,' she admitted. 'But there's a bit of me that can't help thinking, what if?'

'Which is only natural. But you'll have the best medical attention, I promise you. I'll look after you.'

'And that scares me, too. I'm used to being independent, Lorenzo. I don't want to be wrapped in cotton wool.'

'Noted,' he said gently, 'but at the same time I hope you'll understand that I want to keep you and the baby safe.'

'Because the baby might be your heir?'

'No. Because the baby's *ours*,' he corrected.

'Thank you. And thank you for believing me.' She hugged him back.

'Indi, you're not a liar and anybody who meets you would know that within about two seconds.' He stroked her hair. 'I can't believe we're going to be parents. It's…' He couldn't find the right words to explain how overwhelmed he felt.

'I'm sorry,' she said, sounding miserable.

'Don't be. It's not a bad thing. I'm terrified—but it's awesome, too, and I want to jump up and down and tell the whole world that I'm going to be a dad.'

She looked panicked. 'I'm not ready to tell the world.'

'Not until at least twelve weeks,' he reassured her. 'And definitely not until you're ready. This one's your call.'

'You're not angry?'

'Of course I'm not.' He smiled and held her closer. 'I'm thrilled. I don't care that our baby wasn't planned. We're going to have a *baby*, Indi. We've made a family. Do you have any idea how amazing that is?'

'Really?' For the first time since she'd told him, she started to look less scared and more like the sparky, independent woman he'd fallen in love with.

'Really,' he confirmed. 'I have no idea what kind of father I'll be, but I hope I'll be like my grandfather, and give love as well as boundaries.' He wrinkled his nose. 'Maybe slightly less rigid boundaries. And I'll have you to help me do that. You've already made a difference to the way people see me. I'm a better man with you by my side, and I want to be the best husband and father I can possibly be. Right by your side, Indi. No compromises.'

'But—those women in the Ladies'…'

'Were having an idle gossip. And, actually, they're totally wrong.' He took his phone out of his pocket and flicked into a social media site. 'Look. You're trending. There are a lot of influential people talking about you.'

'And how unsuitable I am for the King of Melvante,' she said gloomily.

'No. Look.' He showed her the screen. 'How you're warm and natural. How you're the perfect modern royal, low-key and approachable. How you've brought out a different side in me and they think I'm definitely ready to be king, now. How they hope the stories in the paper are true and that we really are having a secret romance.'

She stared at him, eyes wide, and a tear spilled over her eyelashes. He kissed it away. 'But the most important one for me was my grandfather. Yes, he had doubts. Especially when I told him that you had doubts about our lifestyle. He said that was sensible, but you were probably right. Today, he told me you're still sensible, but you're totally wrong about us. He thinks you'll fit in just fine, and that you're exactly what I need. Someone who'll have my back, who'll tell me things straight, and who—most importantly—will love me as much as I love you.' He kissed the tip of her nose. 'Indi, I want to marry you. I brought you over here to introduce you to my country and because I hoped you'd see that, although I have duties, I'm not just a king-to-be. I'm a man. I love you, and I want to be with you. Not because of the baby, but because of *you*.' He shifted so that she was sitting on her own, and dropped to one knee in front of her. 'I don't have a ring, but that's probably a good thing because it means we get the fun of choosing one together. But I'm asking you first and foremost as a man, and only secondly as the future King of Melvante—will you marry me, Indi? Will you love me, and let me love you all the way back? Will you make a real family with me?'

She dropped to her knees next to him and wrapped her arms round him. 'Yes. Most definitely yes.'

EPILOGUE

TWO MONTHS LATER, the enormous cathedral at Melvante was standing room only.

The previous month, they'd celebrated the coronation of King Lorenzo the Third.

The PR team at the palace had outdone themselves and organised Lorenzo and Indigo's wedding in the shortest possible time. European royalty and heads of state had managed to switch things round in their diaries, and the streets were packed with people eager to catch a glimpse of the new bride and groom.

'You look amazing,' Lottie said, making a last adjustment to Indigo's veil.

'Thanks to Sally.' Her friend's clever dressmaking had managed to hide the bump of the eighteenth week of Indigo's pregnancy. 'And you look amazing, too.'

'Don't. I'll start crying, and then you will, and Lorenzo will throw me in the dungeons for making you cry on your wedding day.'

'I'm not crying,' Indigo said. 'I've never been happier.'

'I'm so glad.' Lottie hugged her, then made a noise of annoyance and fussed with her dress again. 'That's better.'

A carriage drawn by white horses—or, as King Geek had informed her, 'matched greys'—took Indigo to the cathedral.

'Ready?' Gus asked at the door.

'Ready.' She took his arm. 'This is the best day of my life.'

'Just as it should be.' He smiled at her and guided her through the front door of the cathedral, and the organist began to play the beautiful piece of music that Lorenzo had written for her.

The traditional red carpet led all the way to where Lorenzo was waiting for her at the aisle. And instead of cut flower arrangements on the ends of the pews, there were roses in pots, in a rainbow of colours. Half of them had been given by specialist rose-growers, and the other half had been given by ordinary people from their gardens; after the wedding, the roses were going to make a new garden at the palace. And right at the altar was one grown by Lorenzo's grandfather and named after Lorenzo's grandmother.

As Gus delivered her to the altar, Lorenzo looked at her and mouthed, 'You look amazing and I love you.'

'I love you, too,' she mouthed back.

The bishop smiled at them. 'Dearly beloved, we are gathered here...'

And Indigo knew that from now on, it was going to be just fine.

* * * * *

Mills & Boon® Hardback

August 2014

ROMANCE

Zarif's Convenient Queen	Lynne Graham
Uncovering Her Nine Month Secret	Jennie Lucas
His Forbidden Diamond	Susan Stephens
Undone by the Sultan's Touch	Caitlin Crews
The Argentinian's Demand	Cathy Williams
Taming the Notorious Sicilian	Michelle Smart
The Ultimate Seduction	Dani Collins
Billionaire's Secret	Chantelle Shaw
The Heat of the Night	Amy Andrews
The Morning After the Night Before	Nikki Logan
Here Comes the Bridesmaid	Avril Tremayne
How to Bag a Billionaire	Nina Milne
The Rebel and the Heiress	Michelle Douglas
Not Just a Convenient Marriage	Lucy Gordon
A Groom Worth Waiting For	Sophie Pembroke
Crown Prince, Pregnant Bride	Kate Hardy
Daring to Date Her Boss	Joanna Neil
A Doctor to Heal Her Heart	Annie Claydon

MEDICAL

Tempted by Her Boss	Scarlet Wilson
His Girl From Nowhere	Tina Beckett
Falling For Dr Dimitriou	Anne Fraser
Return of Dr Irresistible	Amalie Berlin

ROMANCE

A D'Angelo Like No Other	Carole Mortimer
Seduced by the Sultan	Sharon Kendrick
When Christakos Meets His Match	Abby Green
The Purest of Diamonds?	Susan Stephens
Secrets of a Bollywood Marriage	Susanna Carr
What the Greek's Money Can't Buy	Maya Blake
The Last Prince of Dahaar	Tara Pammi
The Secret Ingredient	Nina Harrington
Stolen Kiss From a Prince	Teresa Carpenter
Behind the Film Star's Smile	Kate Hardy
The Return of Mrs Jones	Jessica Gilmore

HISTORICAL

Unlacing Lady Thea	Louise Allen
The Wedding Ring Quest	Carla Kelly
London's Most Wanted Rake	Bronwyn Scott
Scandal at Greystone Manor	Mary Nichols
Rescued from Ruin	Georgie Lee

MEDICAL

Tempted by Dr Morales	Carol Marinelli
The Accidental Romeo	Carol Marinelli
The Honourable Army Doc	Emily Forbes
A Doctor to Remember	Joanna Neil
Melting the Ice Queen's Heart	Amy Ruttan
Resisting Her Ex's Touch	Amber McKenzie

0714 GEN STD LP

Mills & Boon® Hardback

September 2014

ROMANCE

The Housekeeper's Awakening	Sharon Kendrick
More Precious than a Crown	Carol Marinelli
Captured by the Sheikh	Kate Hewitt
A Night in the Prince's Bed	Chantelle Shaw
Damaso Claims His Heir	Annie West
Changing Constantinou's Game	Jennifer Hayward
The Ultimate Revenge	Victoria Parker
Tycoon's Temptation	Trish Morey
The Party Dare	Anne Oliver
Sleeping with the Soldier	Charlotte Phillips
All's Fair in Lust & War	Amber Page
Dressed to Thrill	Bella Frances
Interview with a Tycoon	Cara Colter
Her Boss by Arrangement	Teresa Carpenter
In Her Rival's Arms	Alison Roberts
Frozen Heart, Melting Kiss	Ellie Darkins
After One Forbidden Night...	Amber McKenzie
Dr Perfect on Her Doorstep	Lucy Clark

MEDICAL

A Secret Shared...	Marion Lennox
Flirting with the Doc of Her Dreams	Janice Lynn
The Doctor Who Made Her Love Again	Susan Carlisle
The Maverick Who Ruled Her Heart	Susan Carlisle

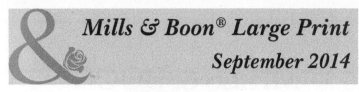

Mills & Boon® Large Print

September 2014

ROMANCE

The Only Woman to Defy Him	Carol Marinelli
Secrets of a Ruthless Tycoon	Cathy Williams
Gambling with the Crown	Lynn Raye Harris
The Forbidden Touch of Sanguardo	Julia James
One Night to Risk it All	Maisey Yates
A Clash with Cannavaro	Elizabeth Power
The Truth About De Campo	Jennifer Hayward
Expecting the Prince's Baby	Rebecca Winters
The Millionaire's Homecoming	Cara Colter
The Heir of the Castle	Scarlet Wilson
Twelve Hours of Temptation	Shoma Narayanan

HISTORICAL

Unwed and Unrepentant	Marguerite Kaye
Return of the Prodigal Gilvry	Ann Lethbridge
A Traitor's Touch	Helen Dickson
Yield to the Highlander	Terri Brisbin
Return of the Viking Warrior	Michelle Styles

MEDICAL

Waves of Temptation	Marion Lennox
Risk of a Lifetime	Caroline Anderson
To Play with Fire	Tina Beckett
The Dangers of Dating Dr Carvalho	Tina Beckett
Uncovering Her Secrets	Amalie Berlin
Unlocking the Doctor's Heart	Susanne Hampton

0814 GEN STD LP

MILLS & BOON®

Why shop at millsandboon.co.uk?

Each year, thousands of romance readers find their perfect read at millsandboon.co.uk. That's because we're passionate about bringing you the very best romantic fiction. Here are some of the advantages of shopping at www.millsandboon.co.uk:

* **Get new books first**—you'll be able to buy your favourite books one month before they hit the shops

* **Get exclusive discounts**—you'll also be able to buy our specially created monthly collections, with up to 50% off the RRP

* **Find your favourite authors**—latest news, interviews and new releases for all your favourite authors and series on our website, plus ideas for what to try next

* **Join in**—once you've bought your favourite books, don't forget to register with us to rate, review and join in the discussions

Visit **www.millsandboon.co.uk**
for all this and more today!